NOT ANOTHER BILLIONAIRE

Not Another Romance Novel

R.L. KENDERSON

Not Another Billionaire
Copyright © 2021 by R.L. Kenderson
All Rights Reserved

ISBN-13: 978-1-950918-43-0

Editor: Jovana Shirley, Unforeseen Editing, www.unforeseenediting.com
Cover image:
Photographer: GoldenCzermak, FuriousFotog, www.onefuriousfotog.com
Model: Hank Meyer
Designer: R.L. Kenderson at R.L. Cover Designs, www.rlcoverdesigns.com

No part of this book may be reproduced or transmitted in any form or by any means, electronic or mechanical, including photocopying, recording, or by any information storage and retrieval system without the written permission of the author, except for the use of brief quotations in a book review.

This book is a work of fiction. Names, characters, places, and incidents either are products of the author's imagination or are used fictitiously. Any resemblance to actual persons, living or dead, events, or locales is entirely coincidental.

Not Another Billionaire

Chapter One
TESSA

I ENTERED the restaurant and spotted one of my good friends and new business partner, Alexis. I was happy to see that she was the only one who had arrived so far.

Tonight was the monthly dinner I had with my six friends from high school. Alexis, Bree, Paisley, Pru, Elizabeth, Isabelle, and I had been friends since our freshman year, and every fourth Wednesday, we met up for dinner. If we didn't plan our get-togethers so far in advance, we would never find the time for all seven of us to be free.

"Hey," I said, sliding into my seat. "I have some news."

Alexis perked up. "You do?"

"Yes, I got a call from the temp agency today. They offered me a position that will last twelve weeks, and the pay is awesome."

Alexis and I had been working on opening up our own bakery and café, but it was easier to say you were going to do something than to actually do it.

We had found the perfect location. It was brand-new and still under construction, but any day now, it was going to be available to buy. The only problem was, Alexis and I didn't have as much money saved as we'd like to.

"Ooh...what are you going to do?"

I bit my lip before spitting it out. "I got a temp job as the assistant to the CEO of a huge advertising agency." And because they were huge, they could afford to pay me very well.

Alexis's face fell. "So, you're going to be the right-hand woman to a rich guy for three months? You're going to hate it. I can't let you do this."

She knew how much I didn't like being around rich people. I'd had an experience that still left a bad taste in my mouth to this day. But I was an adult now, and it was only temporary. I had previously run the office of a small legal firm that included three lawyers, two paralegals, and two receptionists. I could be the assistant to one filthy rich guy.

What I wasn't going to share with Alexis was, I was keeping my fingers crossed that he wasn't a stuck-up jerk with an ego too big to fit through the door. I wasn't expecting someone nice and friendly, but I was hoping for polite and reasonable.

I raised my brow and gave her a look. "Let me, huh?"

"You know what I mean. I know you're doing this because I haven't put together my half of the money yet." She looked away. "I'm already failing as a business partner."

"You stop saying that. It is not your fault your ex-husband is an asshole."

When Alexis and her husband had gotten divorced, as part of their decree, her ex was supposed to sell their house and split the proceeds with Alexis. Their shared home was quite large and would bring in a good amount of money, even with it split between the two of them. Meanwhile, Alexis had been living in a two-bedroom apartment since the divorce even though she could afford more because she was saving for our business. Unfortunately, without her half of the house, she didn't quite have enough to put toward the down payment of the shop. She probably would have had more saved if she hadn't had to spend so much on a divorce lawyer to get out of her awful marriage.

But that was where I wanted to help. Alexis could always pay me back, even though she wouldn't have to, once our bakery was up and running and we were making money.

"I can't help it, sure, but I was the one who married him."

"*Eh.* Win some, lose some."

Alexis chuckled and pushed me away with her elbow. "I think it's more than that, but thank you."

"You're welcome. This job isn't forever, and once it is over, who knows? Maybe your old house will be sold, and we'll just have extra money to buy stuff for our business."

"I like the way you think." She put her head on my shoulder. "You're a good friend."

"I like to think so," I joked.

The door to the restaurant opened, and the rest of our friends walked in as Alexis lifted her head.

"Hey," Bree said, taking a seat beside me. "When did you two get here?"

"I asked Alexis to meet a little early, so I could tell her about my new temp position."

"Ooh, do tell," Paisley said, taking her seat.

Before I could say anything, Alexis told our friends, "She's going to be working for some billionaire at a big advertising agency. She's going to hate it."

"It won't be that bad," I protested.

Isabelle shrugged. "She used to work for lawyers. It can't be any worse."

"Yeah, but those lawyers weren't rich," Pru pointed out.

Pru was right. All of them lived comfortably, but they weren't swimming in money. It was one of the reasons I'd liked working for them. They were down-to-earth and had integrity—unlike some lawyers who were caught up in the number of zeros after a dollar sign.

"*But,*" Alexis added, "she'll not just be working for his company; she'll be working as his assistant. She'll have to talk to him every day and pretend that she likes him."

My friends made sounds of sympathy and looked at me like they felt sorry for me.

"Hey," I objected. "I don't think it will be that hard for me to fake it even if I actually don't like him. I am not a mean person. And that's assuming I don't get along with him. I haven't even met the guy yet."

"But we know how you feel," Elizabeth added.

"You are all making a way bigger deal out of this than it is. My childhood experience wasn't that bad."

"Childhood *trauma*," Pru corrected. "And just because some people might have had it worse than you, that doesn't mean it still didn't affect you."

"Yeah, I know. Okay, so some asshole rich kids used to make fun of me. I highly doubt my new boss is going to do the same thing. I don't know how old he is, but to be the CEO, he's probably in his fifties. Now, we all know men can be immature, but I'm sure he's better than a bunch of high schoolers."

Bree smiled sympathetically. "I suppose he won't tease you. At least, he won't if he knows what's good for him."

The server came over then and took our drink orders and handed out menus. It was a relief for me because I didn't want to talk about my past anymore.

After he left, Pru asked, "I don't think you mentioned the name of the company. How do you know they make a lot of money?"

"It's the Bradford Group. And I'm not sure how they make a lot of money, but they are sure paying me like they do."

"Ooh, hold on. I'm going to look it up," Bree said.

"What do they even do there?" Paisley asked.

"I'm guessing they make advertisements for companies," I said.

"No shit, Sherlock. I meant, what type of companies?"

"Honestly, as long as I get paid and my boss isn't a complete asshole, I don't care who their clientele is."

Bree raised her hand. "Okay, so the Bradford Group was started...twelve years ago and has quickly risen to be the largest advertising agency in the Midwest." She gasped and looked up at me. "What is the name of your new boss?"

"Uh...crap...I can't quite remember." That was probably something I should learn before I showed up on Monday.

"Is it Seth Crawford?"

I snapped my fingers. "That's it."

Bree's eyebrows rose as she read the next line. "Not only is Seth Crawford the CEO, but he is also the founder and owner." She squinted. "Actually, he was a *cofounder* with some guy name John Bradley." She laughed. "I get it. Bradley plus Crawford equals Bradford." She kept reading a little bit more and shrugged. "The Bradley guy is not mentioned again, so I think it's safe to assume that Seth Crawford is the head honcho."

"Oh no," Alexis said. "Your new boss is such an asshole that he drove his business partner away."

"No, he didn't," I said, but inside, I was actually starting to worry. CEO *and* owner. And what if he really was a dick no one wanted to work with?

"Stop scaring Tessa," Pru said. "She's not marrying the guy. She's going to work for him for three months. And there is this little thing called quitting."

I smiled at Pru. "Thank you for putting it into perspective."

"You're welcome."

"It also says something about his parents, Stuart and Deedee, and his brother, Declan. That's a good sign, I think," Bree added.

"I agree. He hasn't ostracized his family, so maybe he didn't scare away his partner," I said. "And before this temp job is even up, Alexis and I will have enough money to put a down payment on our building. Even if I quit, like Pru said, whatever money I make will be worth my time."

"I agree," Bree said. "I'm so happy for you both. Once your place is open, I'm going to be there every day, buying Alexis's baked goodies."

Alexis shifted in her seat. "Thanks, Bree. But if my ex would sell our house, we'd have a nice cushion to actually buy things for our business."

"Is there anything you can do to move it along?" Elizabeth asked.

"Ask my lawyer to pressure him. But that's just more money being taken away from the bakery."

"Let's give the jerk a few more months," I said, not wanting Alexis to spend more money on her ex-husband than she already had. "If nothing happens by then, we'll talk to your lawyer. But we're doing good for now, and I have high hopes for this temp position."

"Thank you."

The server returned with our drinks, and after he left, Pru raised her glass. "Cheers to Tessa's new job and to you ladies being one step closer to getting your new bakery up and running."

As we all picked up our glasses, Alexis smiled. "And let's not forget the United She-Woman Single Ladies with Our Vibrators So We Never Have Another Bad Date or Experience Romance Again Because Men Suck Club."

I tilted my head to the side. "Can we call ourselves that with Bree now in a relationship with my brother?"

"Yes," Bree said. "I am still a founding member after all. And Zack and I are just dating. We're not married or even engaged. Technically, I'm still single."

I snorted.

She scowled at me. "What?"

I gave her my best innocent eyes. "Nothing."

"I don't believe you."

I wouldn't either if I were her because she was in denial. Zack had gone to a trade show last week, and he'd missed her so much that he asked her to move in with him. Bree hadn't said anything to the rest of us, but it turned out, my brother had a big mouth because he'd told me they were already house-hunting. I was letting her sit with her news for a bit because I knew she wanted to take things slow and was probably embarrassed to admit that she was taking such a big step. But she couldn't help it. She and Zack were crazy about each other.

Schooling my expression, I said, "You're right. Technically, you are still single. And we're all still friends." I raised my glass. "So, cheers to everything we already said."

We clinked our glasses and took a drink.

Alexis turned to me. "Please remember, you are more important than our business. If you hate it there, please quit."

"I agree," Pru said. "If push comes to shove, we'll start an online charity."

I grimaced. I did not want to be someone's charity case.

"Everybody, it'll be fine. It's twelve weeks. What's the worst that can happen in twelve weeks?"

Chapter Two

TESSA

MONDAY MORNING, I walked into the tall metal building in the middle of downtown Minneapolis. I'd forgotten to tell my friends that this was the other downfall to the job. Driving around downtown wasn't easy, and parking was almost always a nightmare. My last job had been in a suburb with a nice parking lot attached to the building. Thankfully, there was a parking garage close to the office building, so I didn't have to go too far.

I headed to the security desk at the front. Even though the Bradford Group was a big business, they only used one floor, and the other floors belonged to other businesses. It made me feel a little better about being at this intimidating location.

"Hello. How may I help you?" the polite gentleman in a security uniform said from behind the desk.

"I am starting a job at the Bradford Group today."

He clicked something into his computer. "Your name, please?"

"Tessa Archer."

He scanned his screen. "Ah, there you are. Oh, it looks like you are only here temporarily."

"Yes. I'm filling in as Mr. Crawford's assistant."

The guard's eyes rounded. "Wow. The big man himself."

Oh shit. That didn't seem like a good response. Why was the guy so wide-eyed?

"Yes, the CEO himself." I leaned in. "Is there something I should know before I start my first day?"

The guard shook his head. "Oh, no. I have nothing to say."

That sounded like he had something very interesting to say but didn't want to get in trouble.

I sighed. I hoped I wasn't going to immediately regret this decision. The dollar amount was enticing for my business plans, but I didn't need any workplace drama.

"Okay then. Do I need anything before I go up?"

"One second, please." He shuffled some papers around on his desk until he found what he was looking for. "Here is your temporary pass. Once you're up there, they will take your picture and give you a permanent ID that you can use for the elevators." He waved the white plastic card in his hand. "This will be deactivated after twelve hours, so make sure you get the ID; otherwise, you'll be stopping here again tomorrow."

I held out my hand. "Got it."

The guard slapped the card down. "Have a good first day. And good luck."

"Thanks," I said, heading toward the staff elevators.

Once I reached the eighth floor, there was another reception desk right at the front.

How many people do I have to go through?

The two women greeted me with smiles, and I explained who I was all over again.

"Oh, thank God you are here," one of the receptionists —a blonde woman—said with way too much relief on her face.

Uh-oh. This seemed like another red flag.

The other receptionist—a brunette—clasped her hands together, as if she were praying. "Yes, the last two weeks have been awful."

"Uh…I'm not sure I want to work here if it's that bad," I told them. I was only half-joking.

They bolted around the corner and took my arms.

"No, no, it's not horrible. Let us show you to your cubicle, and then we'll take you directly to HR to get your security badge," the blonde woman said.

"I don't even know your names."

"Oh, I'm Rhonda," the brunette said, "and that's Colleen."

"That's great. I'm Tessa, and I am perfectly capable of walking under my own power."

They both laughed and let go of my arms while I resisted the urge to spin around and make a dash toward the elevators.

After Rhonda and Colleen showed me to my cubicle, they took me by the break room and then HR. I had a new badge that was really just a white rectangle to give me access to the building. When I went back to my desk, it was only after I sat that I realized they hadn't introduced me to my new boss.

I stood up and looked around for someone to give me guidance. Technically, I was out in the main area with the assistants and additional people who didn't get their own private space. But Mr. Crawford's office was in the back and around a corner, so I was secluded from the others and had some privacy.

Mr. Crawford's door was closed, but I could see light coming from underneath, so there was a good chance he was in there. But he might be one of those people who didn't want to be disturbed if their door was closed. One of the lawyers I'd worked with at my old job was like that. We'd all known not to even knock unless it was an absolute emergency.

I finally resigned myself to going back up to the front to find either Colleen or Rhonda when something in my peripheral vision caught my attention.

It was a man wearing a white tank top, a pair of black gym shorts, and a sheen of sweat. He looked to be early to mid-thirties with dark blond hair, styled in a fauxhawk, and a beard.

At first, I thought maybe he was a messenger, but he

didn't have anything with him, except a water bottle and a look of determination as he headed for my new boss's office.

I didn't know what to do. Did I let him go? Did he even belong here?

He sure didn't look like he belonged in an office building, but what if he was Mr. Crawford's son?

I had thought of Mr. Crawford as being in his late fifties to early sixties, making this man too old, but I could have been wrong.

And if I only asked him who he was, I couldn't get fired for that. *Right?*

I bolted over to him so fast that he almost ran into me, but I didn't want him to walk into the office, unannounced.

"Hello, sir," I said. "May I help you?"

He took a step back and looked at the door, which was now behind me. "I don't think so. Can I ask who you are?"

"I'm Mr. Crawford's assistant. It's my first day, and I apologize, but I'm unfamiliar with his clients."

I was pretty sure this guy wasn't a client, but it was the politest thing I could call him.

He raised an eyebrow. "Can I get your name?"

I cringed inside. Wanting someone's name was usually a bad sign. He probably wanted it, so he could complain about me later.

"Tessa," I answered reluctantly.

Nodding, he flipped open the lid to his water bottle and took a long drink.

It was then that I noticed this man was built well.

Broad shoulders, nice biceps, and I would bet five hundred dollars that he had a six-pack under that tank top of his because his legs were thickly muscled. When I brought my eyes back up, I didn't miss the bulge in the front of his black shorts either. The man was clearly not aroused, yet I could see a faint outline of his penis anyway.

I plucked the front of my shirt. All of a sudden, it felt warm in there.

The sound of the man's water bottle clicking closed jolted me back to the present.

"So, Tessa, did you happen to Google the Bradford Group before you started?"

This felt like a quiz.

"Just a little." I mean, it was my friend, but it still counted, right? "I know this company was started twelve years ago," I said with a smile to show him I had done my homework.

I didn't know who this guy was yet, but he must have some serious clout with my new boss if he was asking me questions like this.

But this guy didn't seem to be impressed with my answer. "Did you happen to look at any images during your Google search?"

Oh no, this guy had to be Mr. Crawford's son. Or what if he's Mr. Crawford's lover? Or best friend?

"No," I finally admitted.

"Do me a favor."

Do I have to?

He raised his brow.

"Okay."

But if he asked me to go and fetch him coffee just to prove he was more important than me, I was out of there. I didn't care how much they planned on paying me.

That was a lie. I would totally get this unknown person coffee if I had to. I just wouldn't like it and would definitely be complaining to my friends later.

"I assume you have a smartphone."

I nodded. "Yes."

"I want you to look up *Bradford Group, Seth Crawford*. And then click on Images."

I pointed over at my desk. "I have to—my phone is—" I cleared my throat and held up my finger. "Give me one moment."

I left my spot that blocked him from entering my boss's office, wondering if he'd make a break for it but he stayed where he was.

I found my phone in my purse and searched exactly what he'd asked me to. Once the search results came up, I clicked over to Images...and was flooded with pictures of the guy standing a few feet away from me, only he had on a suit and jacket on my phone.

My mouth dropped open, and I slowly lifted my gaze to his.

I had royally fucked up because he wasn't Mr. Crawford's son, or lover, or best friend.

"Can I go into my office now?"

He was Mr. Seth Crawford, the big man himself.

I tried to apologize, but only a squeak came out, so I simply nodded.

As soon as he was inside and the door was closed, I collapsed in my chair.

I was going to be fired, and I had barely started.

Chapter Three

AFTER I SHOWERED and changed into my suit, it was time to find my new assistant. I figured she'd probably been stewing in the aftermath of our first interaction for long enough.

I sat behind my desk and pushed the intercom button on my phone as I looked at the information the temp agency had sent over to me.

"Yes, sir?" my new assistant's voice answered.

I cringed. I hated being called sir. That title reminded me of my first boss. I still loathed him to this day. He was an arrogant piece of shit, and if I never thought of him again, it would be too soon. Then again, he was the reason I'd started my own company, but I refused to give him any credit.

"Ms. Archer, can you come in here, please?"

A few seconds later, there was a knock at my office door, and Tessa Archer walked in. She had shoulder-length wavy, dark hair with blue-gray eyes. She was slightly taller than average and heavier than what society deemed beautiful. She might be one of those women who called herself fat even though my ex-girlfriend had explained to me that *fat* was not a bad word and women were trying to reclaim it.

Either way, I saw her as voluptuous and sexy. Her hips were as wide as the Missouri River, and I, for one, found it hot as hell. I had to remind Little Seth that she was my employee and not to be messed with. I had never fraternized with a coworker or employee, and I wasn't about to start now.

She sniffed the air, and I realized she probably smelled my body wash.

"I have my own bathroom with a shower," I explained. "It's nice for when I come into work very early and want to get a workout in mid-morning."

She smiled hesitantly, seeming to have received my message about why I had come into the office, looking like I did.

My new employee squared her shoulders. "I apologize for not recognizing you. It was uncalled for, and I should have done my research better. I shouldn't have assumed anything."

I actually liked that she hadn't known who I was when I first walked in. It was the most fun I'd had at work in a long time. I wasn't famous by any means, but everyone in the office —if not the whole building—knew who I was, and sometimes, it got old. I would see my employees talking to one another, but the second they saw me, they'd snap to attention as if I were a drill sergeant and they were my new cadets. That was too harsh of a description. They would smile and say hi to me, but I still often felt like I was the mean, big boss.

I wished I could explain to them that I didn't care if they socialized as long as they got their work done. I used to be one of them, and I would be lying if I said I worked every second of my eight-hour workday. I understood the importance of people enjoying their jobs, and that included making friendships with coworkers. Employees were more likely to stay longer and work harder if they liked their careers.

But I also couldn't be seen as a softie or that I was trying to be one of their friends. While most people were decent, there were some who would try to take advantage or spread the wrong message. And it was better to be seen as too hard than too soft.

"Please sit," I said.

"Is this where you fire me?" she asked after taking her seat.

I raised my brow. "For what?"

"Being rude and not allowing you in your own office."

"Did any projects get delayed?" I asked.

She frowned. "No."

"Was a client insulted?"

"No."

"Was anyone hurt?"

"No," she answered again.

"Then, it's hardly worth firing someone over, especially someone who's not going to be here for long."

"Thank you, sir."

"You can call me Seth or Mr. Crawford."

"Thank you, Mr. Crawford. You can call me Tessa."

Surprisingly, I found myself disappointed that she hadn't called me Seth even though I really hadn't expected her to.

"I'll call you Tessa if you call me Seth." I wasn't sure why I'd insisted on her using my first name, but it felt right, and my gut wasn't wrong when it came to business. Most of the time anyway.

She seemed to consider this. "Okay. Deal."

I smiled at my small victory. "Did you get a security badge?"

"Yes. And I was shown the break room but not much else."

"I can show you around later, if you'd like."

"That would be nice."

"Also, Jill should have left you everything you need to know."

"Jill?"

I smiled. "My assistant."

"Right. Sorry."

"Anyway, she was supposed to have left you instructions and a list of job responsibilities."

"I did find that. I just started to look through it when you called me in here."

"Good," I said with a nod. "Do you have any questions for me?"

"No, Mr. Crawford. I mean Seth."

"If you do, please let me know."

She nodded, but I could tell by her demeanor that I was going to be the last person she asked about anything around here.

My phone lit up, and I heard it ring in the other room. It rang a second time before Tessa's eyes got big and she jumped up from her chair.

"Oh my God, that's me."

I pursed my lips to hold in my laugh as she ran out my door.

That was the second time today she had made me smile, and I'd only been around her an hour.

I absolutely loved my assistant, Jill. She'd been with me for years, and she knew everything I wanted, sometimes even before I did. But Tessa was a breath of fresh air that I planned to enjoy spending time with for the next several weeks.

Chapter Four

TESSA

AFTER TRANSFERRING the call to Seth, I collapsed in my chair.

"What is wrong with me?" I whispered to myself.

It was Monday morning, and I'd already messed up in front of my boss twice. I wanted to march into his office and tell him that I wasn't as incompetent as I seemed. I had previously managed an entire office of a small legal firm, and I really could do this job.

But that would make me look desperate and like I was trying to overcompensate for something. Instead, I would just have to work hard and prove to him that I knew what I was doing.

I pulled out the folder I had found earlier. His assistant, Jill, really had given some very good directions on what I needed to do. She'd even left her phone number in case I needed to call her.

Because Jill seemed so organized and this leave of

absence seemed planned, I found it odd that no one had arranged for someone to take over for her while she was gone.

"Hey, Tessa."

I looked up to see Colleen coming my way with a stack of papers.

"Hello."

"How's it going so far?"

I wasn't about to tell her how I'd already screwed up. "It's going."

"Did you meet the boss man?"

"I did. No one told me he was out of the office this morning though."

When I said *no one*, I meant, her and Rhonda, but she didn't seem to pick up on their failure to let me know he wasn't there.

Colleen rolled her eyes and waved her hand. "Oh yeah. He'll come in super early sometimes, before anyone else gets here, to work alone. But he's also kind of a fitness nut, so on those days, he leaves for about an hour in the morning."

"Yeah, I kind of figured that out," I said, but I didn't think she heard me.

She stared off into the distance. "If you're lucky, you get to catch him with his shirt off. He's a gorgeous specimen of a man." She gasped and leaned forward. "One time, Nina from accounting accidentally walked in on him getting dressed and saw everything." Colleen winked at me. "Apparently, our boss doesn't just have big biceps. If you know what I mean."

"Yes, I know what you mean."

"I mean, he's got a huge di—"

I held up my hand. "*I got it.*"

I whipped my head around to make sure our boss—with the apparently huge dick—hadn't heard us. I sighed with relief when I saw his door was closed. The last thing I needed today was for him to hear me gossiping about him.

Colleen wasn't the least bit offended that I had cut her off. She started laughing at me. "You're not a prude, are you?"

That immediately raised my hackles. "No, I am not a prude. But it is my first day, and I don't need to lose this job only a few hours in."

"I suppose." She smiled. "You should come out for drinks with us after work. Then, we can talk about whatever we want."

I really didn't want to. "I'll think about it," I lied. "I might be exhausted after today."

Colleen laughed again. "No, silly, we don't go out on Monday. We go out on Friday."

Looked like I'd have some time to come up with a different excuse.

I recalled the folder in front of me, and rather than give her an answer, I asked, "Say, can I ask you a question?"

"Yeah, what's up?"

I pointed to my desk. "I have all this information from

Mr. Crawford's assistant, and it seems like she knew she'd be leaving for a while."

"Oh yeah, Jill had a baby."

So, she'd definitely known she'd be gone.

"Why didn't she train anyone to take her spot?"

"Oh, she did."

I waited for Colleen to continue, but she didn't.

"And what happened to that person?"

"Oh, Todd couldn't hack it. Jill did have to go on leave a week early, but Todd should have known what he was doing. I'm surprised he lasted two weeks." She lifted up the pile of papers she was holding. "Which is actually what brought me over here." She plopped them down in my hands. "Rhonda and I have been filling in the last two weeks. Here's all the stuff we've been working on for Mr. Crawford."

I set the papers down and started looking through them. I panicked when I realized I had no idea what any of it meant.

"Don't get too stressed out. This first group is letters to send out. Boss man already signed them, and the addresses are at the top. You just need to print off envelopes with the right addresses on them and mail them off. Oh." Colleen held up a finger and pulled her phone from her back pocket. "I have to take this," she said and started backing away.

"Wait! How do I print off envelopes? And what about the other papers in here?"

"You'll do great," she said. She gave me a thumbs-up,

turned around, and left me to fend for myself.

"Thanks, Colleen," I said mockingly.

"Do you always talk to yourself?"

"*Ah,*" I screamed and spun around in my chair to see Seth standing behind me with his hands in his pockets and one blond eyebrow raised.

I had noticed he was tall earlier, but he seemed like a giant with him standing and me sitting. It also put his crotch right in my line of sight, and all I could think about was how he'd looked in his workout shorts and Colleen telling me he had a huge dick.

Great. Let's add thinking about the new boss's massive penis *on the list of what could go wrong on the first day.*

My face felt like it was on fire, but I looked up into his eyes anyway. "No, Colleen was just here. She gave me some work that she and Rhonda haven't finished."

Seth looked over my shoulder. "Well, that is going to have to wait."

"It is?"

"Yes." He looked at his watch. "We have a meeting in ten minutes. So, grab whatever you need to take notes and meet me in the conference room."

"Okay." I was already too embarrassed to ask him where the conference room was.

"Thanks," he said and started to walk away.

I quickly opened a drawer to look for a notepad when he stopped and turned around.

"Tessa?"

"Hmm?"

"You don't have to be embarrassed. Everyone does it."

I gulped. "Does what, sir?" I winced. "I mean, Mr. Crawford. Ugh. Seth. I mean, Seth."

Surely, he couldn't mean everyone checked out his junk, no matter how impressive it was.

Tessa, you did not just describe your boss's penis as impressive.

"Everyone talks to themselves. And if they say they don't, they're lying." He spun around and continued on.

But I didn't have any time to feel relief because he was almost out of sight.

I found paper and a pen and hurried after him. So far, I had mistaken my boss for a delivery guy, forgotten to answer the phone, and checked out his anatomy. I was not going to get lost on my way to the conference room or be late because I couldn't find it.

Chapter Five

SETH

I LEANED FORWARD at the conference table. "Sounds good. Thanks for the updates."

The head of each department packed up their notes and left the conference room.

I spun in my chair to face Tessa. "Would you like a tour of the rest of the floor?"

She looked up from her notebook, where she had been scribbling furiously. "I'm sorry. What did you ask?"

I smiled. "Now that you met the bosses, I thought we'd take a tour of where each department is located."

"That would be nice."

I stood and adjusted my jacket to wait for Tessa to stand as well, but her head was back down with her pen moving across the paper.

"If it helps, Jill brings her laptop to type out notes, and she also records the meetings to save time."

Tessa paused but didn't look up. "I guess I didn't get that far in her instructions."

"Tessa?"

She raised her eyes.

"Get up and come with me. Everyone who was at the meeting is going to send us what we went over anyway."

She sighed. "You could have told me that right away."

Ooh, a little sass. I liked it.

I shrugged. "But then I wouldn't know how you handled meetings." Pushing my hands in my pockets, I nodded toward the door. "Come on. Let me show you around."

"Okay, fine." She made a show of acting like she was doing me a favor, but I saw the smile she was trying to hide.

We started at the opposite end of the floor, farthest from where my office was.

"You were already shown where HR is located, but just in case you need to complain about me, you can come back here."

HR was the only department that was separated from everyone. It had walls and a door to give my employees privacy if they needed it.

I walked a few steps to the first set of cubicles. "Next, we have accounting."

Tessa's eyes widened.

"Something wrong with accounting?"

She quickly shook her head. "Oh, no."

Odd. "Ladies and gentlemen, this is Ms. Archer. She

will be filling in for Jill while she's on her maternity leave. If you need something, contact her."

Tessa greeted everyone, and they returned her hellos.

I continued on. "Next, we have sales." Again, I introduced Tessa, and I did the same with the marketing department.

We were to the middle of the floor and the best part of the office.

"This is the Think Tank." Inside, there were couches, recliners, a hammock or two, and other various things for employees to relax on. "Advertising is often objective, and sitting at a desk or in an office all day can mess with creativity. And that's where this room comes in."

Tessa smiled. "I was wondering what this room was when I was shown the break room."

"Yeah, they're right next to each other since food is another item people like to use to think."

We stepped up to the doorway, where about a dozen employees were sitting. Some of them sat up when they saw me and stopped talking to their coworkers even though the Think Tank had been my idea. I brushed it off—I was the boss after all—and introduced Tessa.

"Next, we have creative development." This part of the floor was not an open floor plan. Instead, there were offices lined up on each side. "This is where the creative department works. I wanted them to have their own offices, but as you can see, every door is open, and half of them are in the Think Tank."

Jayden Jacobson stepped out of his office. "Oh, hi, Seth. I thought I'd heard you."

I smiled politely but didn't give the kid too much attention. He was awesome at his job and came up with some of the best ad copies I'd ever seen. But he was also an arrogant kiss-ass who only cared about himself. If he wasn't so good at what he did, I'd get rid of him. He never actually broke any rules, he was always on time, and all his clients loved him, but he wasn't fooling me. I did hope that his smarmy attitude was because he was still young and that he'd mature and grow out of it.

"Jayden, this is Ms. Archer. She's my assistant for the time being."

Jayden beamed at Tessa, and she smiled back.

I forgot to add that he was good-looking. Unfortunately, the kid knew it.

I was done with him, so I called the rest of the creative department out and introduced Tessa. Everyone said hi, and we moved on.

The last set of offices was where management was located, and since Tessa had already met all of them in the meeting, I took her back to my office and her desk.

When we reached her cubicle, I said, "Be careful with Jayden."

Tessa frowned, looking confused. "How so?"

"He's a little shit."

Tessa's eyes rounded.

"Unfortunately, he's a little shit who is excellent at his

job and is loved by clients. But other than that, I wouldn't trust him any farther than I could throw him."

"What does that have to do with me?"

She wasn't that clueless, was she?

"I saw the smile he gave you. He'll be over here by the end of the day, asking you out."

Her jaw dropped, and she laughed. "He's...he's so young."

"Around twenty-five, I think. I hired him out of college." The kid had also had an impressive GPA.

"He's not as young as I thought, but I'm still older than him. I can't imagine he'd want anything to do with me."

"You know some guys like older women, right? Not that you are old. I already know from the temp agency that I have you beat by quite a few years." I was thirty-six to her twenty-eight. "Anyway, mark my words. He'll be over here by the end of the day, asking you out."

She was smiling, but I could see by the look on her face that she still didn't believe me. "And why would he do that?"

"Jayden thinks he's on the track to management. What he doesn't understand is, he is not management material. At least, not now. But that doesn't stop him from trying to kiss my ass every chance he gets. And if he can romance my assistant to get a one-up, he'll do that."

"Oh." Tessa's face did a one-eighty, and suddenly, she seemed almost sad.

"You don't want to go out with him, do you?"

Her eyes bugged out. She didn't even have to tell me her answer was no.

"Good. He's not worth your time. There are plenty of other men here you'd be better off dating. Unless you have a husband or boyfriend already."

She still had the same expression on her face.

"I'm sorry. I shouldn't assume. There are plenty of men and/or women that you'd be better off dating."

"Um…no, I like men. And I'm very single."

The relief that went through me was unexpected. I wasn't planning on dating Tessa myself, so I didn't know why I would be happy that she liked men and that she wasn't with anyone.

"Just be careful with Jayden. His intentions might have nothing to do with work because he'd be blind not to notice how gorgeous you are, but I still wouldn't trust him."

Tessa sucked in a small breath and held it.

This woman had so many facial expressions, but I didn't get to ask her about it because around the corner came Jayden.

Sometimes, I hated being right.

Chapter Six

TESSA

THE NEXT MORNING, I stopped and got myself two giant lattes on my way to work, and I had to tell myself several times that it was not appropriate to wear sunglasses on the job even if I wanted to hide my bloodshot eyes and the dark bags underneath them.

Yesterday, Seth had been right. Jayden had come over to ask me out, but even if I hadn't been warned, I would have said no.

Jayden had slimy weasel written all over him, and I wanted nothing to do with that kind of man.

I looked over at Seth's office door as I took a seat. My new boss, however, was a different story. It was probably inappropriate that he had called me gorgeous yesterday, except he hadn't been hitting on me. The matter-of-fact way in which he'd said it only made his statement that much more potent to me.

If anyone was attractive, it was my boss. Handsome,

muscular, and rich. He was a lot of women's wet dream. And he'd told me that I was attractive as if everyone told me that on the daily.

Attention from a rich guy was probably why I'd had a nightmare last night—because his money status had reminded me of high school. I'd thought I had escaped my nightmares when they hadn't shown up the night before my new job. Last night, I hadn't been as lucky.

I collapsed in my chair, took a long drink of my caffeine, and tried not to think about my dreams.

They were always some version of the same storyline. I was back at high school. Not my wonderful public school, but the private school my parents had forced me to attend because my father had gotten a job there.

My family was working class and couldn't afford any of the nice clothes, bags, or makeup the other kids had. But none of that seemed to matter when it came to my brother, probably because he was handsome and athletic. He could have shown up in a potato sack, and the jocks would have welcomed him, and the cheerleaders would have wanted to date him.

I, on the other hand, had never been cool. Add in the fact that I was underprivileged and overweight, and I was the perfect recipe for being made fun of.

In my dream, I was either stuck in a classroom or a dead-end hallway, surrounded by other high schoolers, chanting, "Bessa, Bessa, Bessa."

Bessa was their clever way of combining Bessy—aka a cow—and Tessa. Eventually, the dream progressed to where they either shoved me in a closet or a locker. I guessed, in my dreams, the lockers were big enough to fit me.

I always woke up sweaty and panicky. Being trapped in a small space was my worst fear. I didn't know if I was actually claustrophobic because elevators, airplanes, and tunnels didn't bother me, but things like closets and sensory deprivation tanks did. Give me heights, spiders, snakes, and public speaking any day as long as I wasn't stuck in a tiny, confined area.

After I'd woken up at around two this morning, I had tossed and turned, getting small patches of sleep here and there. Today was going to be a long day.

I finished my first cup of coffee, tossed it in the trash can, and went for my second one.

"Have one of those for me?"

I looked over the lid of my cup to see Seth standing in front of me, looking like he'd just walked off the cover of a catalog.

"If I say no, will you fire me, so I can go home and go to sleep?"

Seth shocked me by laughing.

"I guess that's a no?" I asked.

"Sorry, but it's going to take more than that to fire you. I already went long enough without a real assistant to help; I can't afford to lose you now."

"I guess, on that note…" I reached around my computer and pulled out the latte I'd ordered for Seth. "Here you go."

The look of surprise on his face was almost worth it.

"I read the rest of Jill's notes. Large latte, whole or two percent milk, and no flavor shot."

"Thank you. I can't believe you were going to keep this to yourself." He took a sip. "You must really want that nap."

"I didn't sleep very well last night, but I'll survive. I have a date with my bed at seven tonight. At the latest."

"If you want, you can lie down on the couch in my office."

I shifted in my chair. It was a very nice gesture, but it seemed so intimate. I could never sleep with him in the same room. What if I drooled or something? And I couldn't be sure this wasn't a test.

"I have an appointment that I will be gone all afternoon for, so if you decide to use it, it's yours for a few hours."

That solved him watching me drool, but I still wasn't sure if he was testing me.

"Thank you, but I'll be fine."

"Suit yourself." He lifted his cup. "Thanks again for the coffee."

Around lunch, Seth came out of his office, where he'd been all morning. No workout for him today. "Tessa," he said, putting on his suit jacket, "I'm off. I'll be back around four."

He adjusted his sleeves, and I took a second to admire how handsome he looked.

I would probably never get over his hairstyle because it looked more like something a surfer would wear rather than a CEO, but I liked it. I also noticed that I had yet to see him in a tie. I'd only known him two days, but he hadn't worn one in any of his pictures either. I appreciated the no-tie look.

"Only call you if the building is on fire or everyone goes on strike, right?"

Seth looked up and laughed. "Did Jill actually leave that information?"

"Yes."

He smiled like someone who was remembering something fondly. "It's a joke between the two of us. My assistant before her called me for every little thing."

"So, I can call you about something less dramatic than the building burning down?"

"Yes, but please make sure it's important."

"Noted. Have a good afternoon."

"Thank you. You too."

Seth left, and I finished up what I was working on while I ate my lunch. About an hour later, another employee made their way over to my desk.

"Is Crawford in?" the man said.

"No, he has a meeting outside the building all afternoon."

"Okay." He lifted a couple manila folders in his hands.

"Can you put these on his desk? He wanted them by this afternoon."

I stood and took them from the man. "I'll go and set them on his desk right now." The last part of my sentence was incoherent because a huge yawn decided now was the time to come out of my mouth.

The man raised his eyebrows. "Only the second day, and he's already working you too hard?"

I frowned. "How did you know it was my second day?"

He looked at me awkwardly. "We met yesterday when Crawford introduced us."

I laughed nervously. "Right. Sorry. I am tired, but it's not work-related."

"Okay, well, thanks for taking care of that," the man said. He walked backward away from me, and I assumed it was because he was worried I wouldn't put them on Seth's desk.

To show him I was delivering them immediately, I headed for Seth's office. The man was gone before I opened the door.

Seth's desk was clean with everything in place, so I set the folders down in the middle. They would be the first thing he saw when he got back.

When I turned around, my eyes went straight to the couch. I had never wanted to lie down on one so badly before.

Checking the clock on the wall, I noted that it wasn't even two in the afternoon yet. I had two hours before the boss came back. And technically, he had told me I could rest.

I went and grabbed my phone, set my alarm for two thirty—a half hour was all I needed—and I lay down.

I shoved the corner pillow under my head and closed my eyes. I wondered if there was mouthwash in Seth's bathroom that I could use when I woke up, but I barely had time to finish that thought before I fell asleep.

Chapter Seven

SETH

I GOT BACK to work at five thirty. My afternoon meeting had taken longer than I'd thought it would, and I'd had a few errands to run.

When I got up to my floor, it was quieter than when I had left. There were still some people walking around, but most had left for the day. Unless we were working on a huge project on a deadline, I tried to encourage my employees to not overwork themselves. I didn't want them to get burned out and quit.

When I got back by my office, it appeared that Tessa was already gone, and I found myself slightly disappointed she hadn't stuck around. Not that I blamed her.

I glanced over the wall to her cubicle and saw that her computer was on, so maybe she was still around.

Figuring she'd show herself sooner rather than later, I went into my office to get a few things done before I went home for the night. Rob was supposed to get his project to me today, and I wanted to look at it before I left, just in case it needed revising before his meeting tomorrow. I was sure he'd emailed me the information, but I liked paper mock-ups when possible. I was able to catch more issues and get the full impact with paper versus a digital format.

I pulled off my jacket as soon as I walked in. One thing I disliked about being a CEO was having to wear a suit every day. I could admit that I paid good money to get clothes that fit well and were comfortable, but I'd still rather wear jeans and a T-shirt.

With a sigh, I collapsed into my chair, and then I saw her.

Tessa was sleeping on my office couch.

Her back was to me, but I knew it was her by her dark hair and spectacular ass. This morning, I had noted how good she looked in her dark purple dress, and I hadn't forgotten. It was definitely Tessa.

But since I had also noted how tired she was this morning, I opted to not disturb her, and I opened the folders that had been placed on my desk.

I was about halfway through my notes to Rob when I heard a whimper coming from the other side of the room. I looked up to see Tessa shaking her head back and forth.

"No. Please," she mumbled.

Shit. She was having a bad dream.

I got up from my desk and walked over to her. I didn't know if it was better to try to soothe her or to wake her up, so I opted for trying to calm her first. Especially since I had no idea how she'd react to waking up in my office. I sat down by her legs and put my hand on her upper arm.

She stilled, and her breathing evened out some, so it seemed to have worked.

As I was about to get up again, she muttered, "No, no, not again," and rolled onto her back so fast that she kneed me in the side.

The pain in her voice was it for me.

"Tessa, wake up," I commanded.

Her eyes popped open, and she bolted into a sitting position.

She looked visibly shaken, and the color had drained from her face.

"Oh my God, I am so sorry. I didn't—"

I put my hand up because that wasn't important right now. "Are you okay?" I asked.

"I guess that depends."

I frowned. "On what?"

"How much trouble I'm in."

"You're not in trouble. I'm asking if you're okay because you were having a bad dream."

"Oh, that. Yeah, I get nightmares from time to time. It's not a big deal."

I didn't believe that and suspected that was why she had been tired when she came into work this morning.

I stood and held out my hand. "Let me take you home."

"I can't let you do that. I live over a half hour away. Besides, my car is here."

"Where do you live?"

"Shakopee."

It wasn't the closest suburb, but it wasn't the farthest away she could live either.

"It's okay. I live close. Let me take you home."

She eyed me skeptically. "You live close to Shakopee?"

"Close enough," I lied. "Now, let me take you home."

"But then I won't be able to get back here in the morning."

"I'll pick you up."

Her eyes rounded. "Won't that look bad?"

"Why? People commute together to work all the time."

"I'm fine. Really." She swung her legs to the floor, pushed herself to her feet, and immediately swayed.

I grabbed her around the waist. "Whoa. I don't think you're fine."

She looked up at me, and close up, I noticed how beautiful her eyes were. I also noticed how good she felt against me.

I let her go and stepped back. "I'm taking you home. No further arguments," I said in a voice that was firmer than needed. But I was hard now and wasn't in the mood to waste time, having her try to convince me that she was better off driving herself.

She took the time to shut off her computer and grab her things, and we headed to the parking garage in silence.

When we got to my vehicle, she asked, "Is your other car in the shop?"

"My other car?"

"Yeah, I thought you'd drive a sports car or something. At least in the summer."

I laughed. "Tessa, this is a Cadillac Escalade."

"Okay. I don't know what that means, except it's an SUV."

I smiled at her. Escalades weren't the most expensive SUV on the market, but they were up there. "Get in."

Once we were both seated, I handed her my phone. "Type in your address."

Taking my cell from me, she started typing as I made my way out to the street.

I heard my phone ding, and Tessa said, "Oh. *Oh*."

"What?"

She shoved my phone back at me and turned her face away. "I think you should take this back."

"Did you finish typing in your address?"

"No."

"Why not?"

"Because I just saw some stranger's bajingo."

"Bajingo? What's a bajin—" I burst out laughing as I answered my own question.

"It's not funny."

I tried to school my face. "You're right. The fact that you saw what you saw is not funny. But the fact that you called a pussy a bajingo is very funny." I grinned because I couldn't hold it in.

We got to the bottom of the ramp, and since no one was behind me, I quickly grabbed my phone and looked. I sighed when I saw the name and immediately deleted the picture. I put my cell back in Tessa's lap.

"It's safe now. I deleted the pic. Can you tell me which way to turn and finish putting in your address?"

"Go right." She finished typing. "Done. Where should I put it?"

I pointed to the magnet I had on my dashboard. "But before you hang it up, can you find Amy in my text messages?"

"Who's Amy?"

"The woman whose bajingo you just saw," I teased.

Tessa rolled her eyes at me. "You're not funny."

"I believe you already told me something to that effect."

"So, why would I need to find her in your text messages?"

"Two reasons. I'm driving, and you're my assistant. I need you to assist me, so I don't get us into a car accident."

"If you need help sending a dick pic back to her, I quit."

I laughed again. "No. I need you to text her and tell her to stop messaging me."

"Wait, really?" Tessa put the phone down. "But she just sent you an intimate photo. A very intimate photo."

"Yeah. One that I did not ask for."

I had met Amy a couple of years ago at a fundraiser. She'd seemed nice when I first met her, but it was clear she only wanted a rich husband. I had known long ago that I would rather be alone than in a relationship that wasn't based on love.

"Huh."

"What's *huh*?"

"I guess I never thought a guy would turn down something like that."

"Then, you haven't been around the right kind of guys."

She seemed to think on this. "You're right. Anyway, what do you want me to say?"

I rubbed my chin. "If you pursued a guy who wasn't showing you interest, what would make you leave him alone?"

She opened her mouth, and I just knew she was going to tell me that she would never pursue a man who didn't want her.

"Hypothetically," I quickly added.

"Hmm..." She looked down at my phone and typed away. A few seconds later, she hung up my phone on the dash and rubbed her hands together. "And done."

"What did you say?"

"I wrote, *Please stop sending inappropriate photos like this. You are a lovely person, but I am not interested in dating you. However, my grandfather, who saw your picture first, is a widower and would very much like to take you out.*"

"You didn't."

"You're right. I didn't."

I chuckled. "Oh shit, that would have been good though."

She lifted a shoulder. "I thought so. But I didn't want to make your grandpa, even if he's fictional, a dirty old man."

"So, what did you really say?"

"What every woman hates to hear. *I'm sorry, but I'm in a relationship now. Please stop sending me inappropriate photos. Otherwise, I will have to block you.* As a woman, it's never fun to be turned down for someone else."

My phone dinged, and Tessa leaned forward. "Wow. This bitch has balls."

She snatched my cell up without even asking me, and I liked how she was taking charge. A good assistant knew when to do things on her own.

I turned my eyes back to the road, but I heard my camera click, and then Tessa mumbled something.

This time, she practically slammed my phone back down.

"Hey, gentle. It didn't do anything to you."

"Sorry."

"What happened?" I asked as my GPS told me to turn left up ahead.

"She said she didn't believe you, and if you had a woman in your life, you'd show proof." She scoffed. "What kind of woman doesn't believe that? And even if she doesn't, it's apparent by the message that *he doesn't want you, Amy.*"

"Should have gone with the grandpa scenario after all."

I wasn't the least bit surprised Amy would not take a text at face value. "So, did you block her?"

"Nope. I sent her back a picture of my boobs."

This had me almost driving into the curb. "For real?"

"I had to send her proof that you had someone."

"I'm sure just a picture of us smiling with our heads together would have done the trick."

"Oh...I guess I'm still tired." She shrugged. "Oh well. Too late now."

Too late for Amy's eyes and too late for my imagination.

After I dropped Tessa off at her house, I drove back to the city and to my penthouse apartment. I had lied when I told her I lived close, but she would have never let me take her home otherwise. Besides, it wasn't that big of a deal to take her home and pick her up in the morning.

I threw my suit in the laundry, put on a pair of gray sweats, and went to cook a small dinner.

As my food was simmering on the stove, I grabbed my phone. I really did need to block Amy, but first, I needed to delete her message thread and her number from my Contacts list.

When I opened my text messages, I saw that she had messaged back: *Dick*. Out of curiosity, I opened it just to check to see what Tessa had written.

She had indeed actually sent Amy a message about me

having a girlfriend. And she had also sent Amy a picture of her breasts. And then she had not remembered to delete it.

It was ten times sexier than the crotch shot Amy had sent.

I turned off the burner and headed to my room. My hard cock was in my hand before I even reached my bed.

I should not be thinking about my assistant like this, yet I couldn't help myself. One thing was for sure: if I didn't keep myself in line at work, I would be in a world of trouble.

Chapter Eight

TESSA

THE NEXT MORNING, I found myself actually excited to see Seth.

I had gone to bed early, slept without a single bad dream, and woken up, feeling refreshed. Not only was I in a much better mood than the previous morning, I had also enjoyed the ride home last night.

It had been fun to help Seth fend off the Amy woman, and I was impressed that he hadn't taken her up on her offer. He was definitely good-looking and rich enough to sleep with a woman and never call her again, and that woman probably wouldn't even hold a grudge. He could have dropped me off and gotten himself a booty call. But instead, he had asked for my advice on how to let her down in a way that firmly delivered the message.

When I saw Seth pull into my driveway, I rushed outside, so he wouldn't have to wait for me.

"Good morning," I said as I got in and closed the door.

"Morning," he said without even glancing my way.

Someone was in a bad mood, it seemed.

"Everything okay?" I asked.

"Just fine."

"Did Amy text you back last night?"

He tensed up but only for a second.

Maybe he had gone to see her after he dropped me off.

The amount of disappointment I felt was not rational.

"Sorry, it's none of my business," I said.

Just because he had been open with me yesterday didn't mean he felt that way this morning.

"No, it's fine. She called me a dick, and that was that."

I chuckled, and he shot me a look.

"I don't mean to laugh, but it is kind of funny. Do you think she'll leave you alone now?"

He shrugged. "Doesn't matter if she does or not. I blocked her."

I turned away from him and grinned. So, he hadn't gone to see Amy last night. But I couldn't let my pleasure in this information show. I shouldn't even be feeling pleasure about this situation. This was my boss.

"I figured out why I was still sleeping on your couch yesterday. I'd accidentally set my alarm for a.m. instead of p.m. Not that I should have done it in the first place. It was very inappropriate of me to sleep on the job."

"I said that you could. And as long as you get your work done, I don't care what you do on your breaks."

Except I had slept way longer than a simple fifteen-minute break, but I didn't say that out loud. Even though

Seth was speaking to me, he still seemed to be brooding about something. Maybe he hadn't felt like picking me up this morning.

I chewed on my lip. Added to the fact that I'd made him leave work earlier than he planned last night, he might be upset he had driven me home.

It was probably best to leave him alone.

I occupied myself with looking at my phone and scrolling on social media to pass the time, and we got to work sooner than I had expected.

We got out of his vehicle, and he took off as soon as his door was closed.

"I need to get up there. I had planned to finish looking over Rob's stuff last night," he said as he walked away, leaving me to stand there by myself.

So, he had gotten behind on work, and even though he had been the one to insist on driving me home the evening before, I still felt bad. If Seth had asked, I would have even gone into work early today.

Hoping to smooth things over, I walked the two blocks to the nearest coffee shop to get him a latte. When I entered, the sights and smells reminded me of what I was working toward. My own place like this.

So, if my new—yet temporary—boss was a little irritated today, I could deal with it because it was bringing me one step closer to my dream.

By Friday, things at the Bradford Group had shifted into a normal work experience.

There were no more embarrassing moments between Seth and me. I didn't mistake him for someone else, I didn't fall asleep on his couch, and he didn't drive me home again.

And while he wasn't as friendly with me as he had been on Tuesday evening, he wasn't as standoffish as he had been on Wednesday morning.

He was treating me like a normal employee, and I was treating him like my boss.

Late that morning, I had just returned to my desk from the copy machine when my phone buzzed.

> Alexis: What time do you take lunch?

> Me: Between 11:30 and noon. Why?

> Alexis: Was hoping to talk to you during your break.

> Me: I can do that.

I spotted an empty office that I could use to talk to Alexis in private when she called me. I didn't want Seth or anyone else to hear me talking to my friend. She might have bad news.

> Me: Everything okay with the ex?

> Alexis: No. What I mean is, nothing has changed. But it wasn't good to begin with.

> Me: So, you're saying, there could be better news.

> Alexis: LOL. Yes.

> Me: I'll talk to you in about an hour. Sound good?

> Alexis: Sounds perfect.

I set down my phone and went back to work.

I actually lost track of time and didn't look up until I heard, "Tessa?"

It was Rhonda coming around the corner.

I stood. "Yes."

"Were you expecting someone?"

I frowned in confusion.

"Someone named Alexis?"

"Oh, uh, Alexis is my friend."

Rhonda waved behind her, and Alexis popped around the corner.

"Surprise," she said and held up a white box.

I grinned. "I didn't know you were coming here."

She wiggled her hips and smiled as she walked over to me. "That's because I fooled you into thinking that I wanted to talk on the phone."

"Yeah, you did."

I noticed that Rhonda was still there. "Thanks for bringing Alexis over here."

"You're welcome. And don't forget, we're going for drinks tonight."

I froze.

"Colleen said she told you."

"Oh, she did, but I forgot." *Forgot to come up with a good excuse.* "I have plans with Alexis," I said.

Rhonda looked over at her. "Your friend can come too."

Well, crap. What do I say now?

"Sorry, we can't," Alexis said in a disappointed voice that I recognized as fake, but Rhonda probably didn't have a clue. "We have a double date we're going on tonight. Although drinks with the girls sounds much more fun."

I stifled a laugh.

"Maybe next time," Rhonda said.

I only nodded, so I didn't do something inappropriate.

Once she was gone, Alexis and I erupted into laughter.

Chapter Nine

SETH

"YOU ARE SUCH A LIAR," Tessa told her friend. "A double date." She snorted. "I think that goes against the club oath."

"I had to say something," her friend said. "Otherwise, you'd be going out with them tonight." She lowered her chin. "I mean, the last I heard, you didn't want to go, did you?"

"God, no. I just want to go home and relax." Tessa pointed at something. "Now, show me what you brought me."

Her friend looked up and saw me. She blinked a couple of times. "Tessa, I think someone needs something from you."

I stepped out of my doorway. I hadn't meant to listen to their conversation so long, but it had seemed rude to interrupt them. However, now that I'd been seen, I might as well introduce myself.

Tessa spun around. "Mr. Crawford. I was just going to lunch. If that's okay?"

I frowned. "When have I stopped you from going to lunch, *Tessa*?" Putting emphasis on her name might remind her that I wanted her to call me Seth.

She chuckled nervously. "Never. But I didn't know if you needed anything from me before I left."

"Nope. I was actually going to tell you that I was going to lunch myself. I should be back in an hour or so."

Tessa's friend cleared her throat.

"Sorry. Alexis, this is my boss, Seth Crawford." She glanced away and back to me, as if embarrassed. "Seth, this is one of my good friends, Alexis."

Alexis stepped forward and held out her hand. "Good friend *and* business partner."

Hearing the term *business partner* was a temporary blow to the gut, but I quickly recovered. "Business partner?" I asked as I shook her hand.

"Yes." Alexis beamed. "Tessa and I are opening up a bakery and café." She turned and grabbed the white box she had been carrying earlier and opened it toward me. "Would you like to try one? I brought extra in case Tessa wanted to share."

Inside were a dozen cupcakes in a rainbow of colors. The yellow ones were the first to catch my eyes though.

"I should say, would you like to try one, except the lemon cupcakes? Those are Tessa's favorite, and you just might lose a limb if you take them from her."

I looked over at Tessa, who rolled her eyes.

"Yes, they're my favorite, but you made two. I can share, but I'm sure Mr. Crawford would rather have chocolate or peanut butter or something else."

I plucked a lemon one right out of the box. "Nope. Lemon is my favorite."

Tessa's jaw dropped, and Alexis said, "I told you," as she tipped her head toward her friend. "None of our other friends like that flavor much, so she's used to getting them all to herself." She elbowed her friend. "But isn't it nice to find someone else who likes the same thing you do?"

Tessa narrowed her eyes. "As long as he doesn't eat both."

I laughed. "I promise not to touch the other one. But this one definitely belongs to me." I ran my tongue along the top of the cupcake, circling the lemon candy at the tip before sucking it into my mouth. "Mmm." I looked up at Tessa and grinned. "I licked it, so it's mine."

Alexis grabbed Tessa's arm, but neither of them said a word. They both stood there as if they were in shock.

I checked my watch. I didn't have time for any more chitchat. I needed to get going.

"I'd better head out, so I'm not late. Nice to meet you, Alexis." I lifted the cupcake. "Thank you for the dessert." I looked at Tessa. "Like I said, I'll be back in an hour."

I pivoted on my heel and headed for the elevator. Once inside, I took a bite of my cupcake.

It was delicious.

If everything was this good, then Tessa and Alexis might have a shot at opening that bakery and café.

I hoped things worked out better for the two of them than it had for John and me. It was quite the coincidence that I had met Tessa's business partner on the day that I was going to visit mine at the cemetery.

Tessa

Once the elevator doors closed, Alexis finally let go of my arm.

"Oh my God. Did you see the way he—"

"I don't want to talk about it," I interrupted with a hand in the air. "He's my boss."

My boss, who had just licked the fronting on the cupcake like it was a pussy and circled the lemon candy on top like it was a clit before sucking it between his lips.

The tingling between my legs was unnecessary and way out of line. I absolutely could not be thinking about Seth like that.

"Tessa, why didn't you tell me your boss was gorgeous?"

I shrugged. "Is he? I guess so."

Alexis burst out laughing. "You're full of crap."

"I know he's good-looking, okay?" I admitted. "You remember how I told you about the first time I met him?" I hadn't forgotten his thick biceps and muscular body even though I tried to pretend I did. "He looks even better under that suit. It's not fair."

"I can't wait to tell the rest of the group about him."

"No, don't."

Alexis scrunched up her nose. "Why not?"

"I don't know. I just don't want them to tease me. It was already a big deal with my even taking this job."

"They wouldn't tease you."

I sighed. "I know. At least, not a lot. I just don't want to make anything out of it."

"Okay, I won't say a word."

"Thank you." I narrowed my eyes. "Besides, you owe me after giving away one of my favorite cupcakes to someone else."

Alexis had started baking when she was married to her ex-husband as a way to escape the reality of being stuck with him. So, even though it hadn't worked out with him, we would have probably never known she was so good in the kitchen if they'd never been married.

She laughed. "Getting to watch your boss lick the cupcake like it was a vagina was completely worth it. I have no regrets."

I shook my head sadly. "You just had to say it, didn't you?"

"You were already thinking it anyway."

Thinking about it and putting it in my memory bank for later when I was alone with my vibrator.

"We are on a dating strike," I reminded Alexis. "The club."

"Dating, yes. Masturbating, no. Actually...sex, also no."

I clenched my jaw. "You're not having sex with Seth," I said much more firmly than was needed.

Alexis bit her bottom lip and laughed. "Seth, is it? Not Mr. Crawford?"

I lifted a shoulder. "He told me to call him by his first name."

My friend's expression turned serious. "Don't worry. I'm not going to have sex with your boss. I wouldn't do that to you."

"Thank you." I did not even want to imagine how that would affect my work life.

And I didn't want to admit it, but picturing Alexis with Seth put an uncomfortable pit in my stomach.

"I don't promise to not think about him while masturbating though." Alexis grinned.

"You're horrible."

She laughed again and picked up her purse. "Let's go eat. We can talk about handsome men."

"Yes, let's go to lunch. Handsome men can wait though."

I didn't want to think about my boss or his tongue or his tongue on me anymore today.

It's a good thing I'm only here for eleven more weeks. There was no way I could do this job more than that with the inappropriate thoughts I was already having.

Chapter Ten

TESSA

A WEEK LATER, I was settled into my new job. Seth had been in and out of the office all week, so I felt like I had talked to him more on the phone than in person, which was fine with me.

This morning had started out like any other until a couple of employees rushed to the boss's office to see him. They went in and shut the door. I couldn't make out what they were saying, but they got quite loud. I didn't think anyone was in trouble, but something was definitely going on because Seth was on the phone with the door shut the rest of the day.

If I hadn't gone out and gotten him a sandwich, I didn't think he would have even eaten. And I was too afraid to leave my desk in case Seth needed something from me.

It was a little before two o'clock when he threw open his door and shouted, "We're in."

I jumped up from my chair. I had no idea what he was

talking about, but going by the grin on his face, it was good news. "Congratulations."

"I need you to call Jayden, Leeann, Guy, and Tiffany and tell them to come to my office ASAP."

"On it," I said, already reaching for my phone.

Seth turned to go back into his office but stopped halfway and faced me again. "Shit. I almost forgot. Book two tickets to San Francisco for Sunday. First class."

"One-way or round trip?"

"Round trip. Set the return date for Saturday morning. That should be plenty of time."

"Got it."

Seth went back into his office, and I called the four people he had requested. I didn't understand why Seth needed them, but they already seemed to know what was going on.

After hanging up, I pulled up Seth's preferred airline, per Jill's notes. I'd forgotten to ask what time he wanted to leave, but there was only one flight with two first-class seats available anyway. Except, when I got to the information part, I didn't know who the other ticket was for. Seth had called four people over, but he hadn't told me who was going with him.

The office door was open, so I went to the doorway and knocked.

Seth looked up from where he was standing his desk.

"I'm sorry. I forgot to ask, who is going with you to San Francisco?"

When he didn't respond, I continued, "I found two

tickets for Sunday that leaves a little after six in the evening, but I only have about fifteen minutes to get them. Do you need to talk to everyone before deciding?"

Seth stood. "I apologize. Did you have plans on Sunday and next week?"

Oh. Does he expect me to be in the office on Sunday? Or does he think I am going to not do my job because he won't be here?

Either way, I knew trips were a part of the job description and that I might have to work weekends.

I shook my head. "No. I can be available whenever you need me all week."

"Good. Because I need you to put the ticket in your name."

"My name?" I squeaked.

"Yes," he said as he sat back down. "You're my assistant, and I need you to go to San Francisco to assist me. I can't do this by myself."

"Don't you want someone who knows what they're doing to go?"

He laughed. "I need them here." He looked me up and down. "And you seem to know what you're doing just fine."

I didn't think he meant the comment in a sexual way at all, but I felt a pulse between my legs nonetheless.

This attraction was why I didn't want to go to San Francisco alone with him and why I had been fine with talking to him on the phone more than in person. How was

I going to be around him for almost a week with no buffer between us?

He raised an eyebrow. "Is there a problem?"

"Oh, no. No. I will go and book the tickets." I moved to return to my cubicle.

"Oh, Tessa?"

"Yes?"

"Don't forget the hotel too."

"Right."

"And make sure you get me a suite. We're going to need some space to work."

I swallowed hard. *Does that mean he wants me in the same room as him?*

"When you make the reservation, make sure you tell them to put your room close to mine, so you don't have to run around the hotel, going back and forth."

My shoulders sagged. That answered that question.

I went back to my desk just as the four people I had called minutes ago came around the corner. They didn't even glance at me as they headed for Seth's office.

After the door closed, I finished booking the flights and did a Google search for San Francisco hotel suites. Of course, there were a dozen websites that popped up, so I went by reviews and took a guess at which hotel I should call.

With the phone ringing in my ear, I quickly grabbed my cell and sent Alexis a text.

> Me: I just found out I have to go to San Francisco with my boss for almost a week. Just the two of us!

"This is Catherine. How may I help you?"

"Hello. I realize this is last minute, but I need to book one of your suites, starting on Sunday."

"One moment while I look that up."

"Thank you."

I checked my phone while I waited.

> Alexis: Oh my God. That's so quick. Is it for business or pleasure? ;-)

I snorted.

> Me: Of course it's for business.

> Alexis: I know. But a part of me was hoping you'd say it was for both.

I laughed just as Catherine came back on the line.

"It looks like our presidential suite is available. Does that work for you?"

"Yes, please."

"How many nights?"

"Till Friday, so six nights."

"Name?"

"Seth Crawford."

I heard Catherine clacking on her keyboard from the other side of the phone as Alexis texted me again.

Alexis: You know a part of me is hoping you have sex with him since I can't.

Me: Oh my God. I can't have sex with my boss!

Alexis: What if he wasn't your boss?

I thought about this. Seth was hot, and he did things to my body, but he was the richest of the rich and could get any woman he wanted.

Me: Fine. I would let him do dirty things to me. Like really dirty.

Alexis: I knew it!

Me: But it's not going to happen. Even if he wasn't my boss, the man probably has women knocking down his door. He doesn't need me.

Or want me, I was sure.

Alexis: Don't sell yourself short.

Me: I'm not. He's rich and gorgeous. I live comfortably and am pretty at best. Not to mention, my hips put me outside of supermodel territory, which is what he probably dates.

> Alexis: You're gorgeous, but besides that, I have a really good idea.

> Me: Do I dare ask?

> Alexis: Yes.

> Alexis: I'm going to make a dozen lemon cupcakes, and I'll to give you extra lemon frosting for you to "accidentally" spill on your vagina. Then, you can ask him to lick it off you.

I burst out laughing just as Catherine said, "Okay, your room is almost booked. Are you going to be joining him?"

"Yes," I managed to say through my amusement. "I'm sorry for laughing in your ear. My friend just sent me a funny text."

"No worries, miss. It doesn't prevent me from doing my job." I could hear the smile in her voice and appreciated her good nature.

"Thank you."

"You're all set. Is there anything else I can help you with?"

"No, thank you. That is it."

"We'll see you on Sunday. Have a safe trip."

"You too." I laughed again. "I mean, thank you."

I hung up the phone and read my text again.

> Me: Oh my God, you are horrible.

Me: That's not going to happen, but I will take the cupcakes though.

Alexis: How would you get them on the plane?

Me: Now, you're telling me no? It was your idea.

Alexis: That's when I was trying to get you laid.

Me: Thanks…I guess.

Alexis: Do you want me to come over on Saturday and help you pack?

Me: Yes, please. I've never been to California.

Alexis: I'll be over in the morning.

Me: Thank you. You're the best.

Chapter Eleven
TESSA

SUNDAY AFTERNOON, my brother and Bree dropped me off at the airport, so I wouldn't have to leave my car in long-term parking.

Zack popped the back of his SUV and got out of the car with me.

"You don't have to help me," I said as I pulled my carry-on out of the back.

He lifted my suitcase out and set it on the ground. "It's what brothers do."

"Thanks." I gave him a hug.

Zack and I had never been that close, but we'd become closer when he started dating my friend.

"And thank you for the ride."

"Happy to help."

We carried my stuff to the curb, and Bree got out.

With a hug, she said, "Have fun in California. Try to sightsee a little."

"I will. I don't know how busy we'll be with work, but I'm going to try to relax when I can."

She squeezed me again and let go.

I slung my carry-on over my shoulder, grabbed my suitcase handle, and entered the airport.

Seth and I were flying out of Delta, so I made my way over to the check-in area and looked around for him.

When I didn't spot him, I checked my phone to see if I was early. I was right on time, but maybe he was running late.

While I kept a lookout for my boss, I noticed a guy standing about ten feet away. His back was facing me, and he had his head down as he leaned against a pillar. One leg was crossed over the other, and he seemed to be waiting for someone, just like me.

He had on a fitted dark gray T-shirt that showed off the muscles in his back and arms. And his dark jeans looked like they had been made to fit him. His ass was sublime. I sighed, a tad jealous I wasn't going on vacation with him. He was tall, muscular, and I tried not to stare as I waited for him to turn around, so I could see if his front side matched his backside. I also wanted to see who he was going out of town with. Someone as beautiful as him, I imagined.

After about five minutes, I started to wonder if I had come to the wrong area. We had agreed to meet early, so we would have plenty of time to get through security, but I could see the line was outrageously long from where I was standing, and I was starting to worry we'd have to rush.

Even the hot guy wasn't enough of a distraction for my concern anymore.

I pulled out my phone again and found Seth's number.

As the phone rang in my ear, I turned to the hot guy once more. Whoever he was leaving with today hadn't shown up either, and I might as well enjoy his butt for a few more minutes.

He still had his head down, but he shifted enough that I saw his own phone in his hand. He hit a button and lifted it to his ear.

I chuckled as I realized we were both possibly going to be talking to our flying partners at the same time.

"Tessa?" Seth's deep voice sounded in my ear. "Where are you?"

I frowned. I must have gotten our meeting spot wrong. "I'm at the check-in. I thought that's where we were supposed to meet up. Did you need me to meet you somewhere else?"

Hot Guy chose that moment to turn around, and I almost dropped my phone when I saw it was Seth.

Of course, Hot Guy was my boss.

I didn't know why I'd thought he'd be dressed in business attire. It was probably because that was how I always saw him, but it made sense that he was wearing something more comfortable for flying.

And if I'd thought he looked good in a suit, he looked even better in jeans and a T-shirt. I had to resist the urge to lick my lips because the front was just as good as the back.

His tee showed off his muscular chest, and his jeans—dear God—I thought I could see the outline of his package in them even though they weren't tight.

I shifted from one foot to the other and tried to ease the ache in my body as heat washed over me.

I needed to get laid because my boss was looking extra sexy right now.

It didn't help that he grinned as he walked over to me. His smile was sexy too.

"Hey. How long have you been here?"

"A few minutes. I didn't realize it was you over there." I didn't want him to know I'd been ogling his ass for over five minutes.

Seth reached over to me, and I sucked in my breath, wondering what he was going to do to me. A part of me hoped he'd touch me, but he went for my cell and hit the End button.

"I don't think we need to use our phones anymore," he said when I looked up at him in what was most likely surprise.

Surprise that I'd been so mesmerized by him that I forgot to end my call.

"Thanks. I thought I'd already done that," I lied.

"Shall we get going?"

"Yes."

Anything to keep my mind off my sexy boss.

Our check-in was fast, but we spent over forty-five minutes in the security line. After that, we stopped and picked up coffee since we had a four-hour flight and California was two hours behind us.

We were one of the first to board the plane. I pulled out my paperback to read, took the seat by the window, and buckled up. I had to admit, the leg room in first class was pretty nice. Seth sat in the aisle seat with his laptop.

"Are you going to work?" I asked, pointing to his computer.

"Maybe. I had the team brainstorming all weekend, and I figured I could look over a few things."

"You know, you never explained to me why we're going to San Francisco. I guessed by all the excitement on Friday, it was something big, but I must have missed the memo on what exactly was going on."

The corner of his mouth turned up in a half-smile, almost as if he had a secret. He leaned closer to me, and I caught a hint of his cologne. I almost closed my eyes to savor his smell, but then I would have looked ridiculous. However, I couldn't look in his eyes, so I ended up staring at his shirt pulled over his muscular chest instead.

This flight was going to last forever.

"Paragon fired their ad company," Seth said in a low voice.

This news was big enough to snap me out of my fantasies. Paragon was one of the biggest electronics and appliance companies in the world. They made Android phones, televisions, computers, washers and dryers, kitchen appliances, and a host of other things. I might not have been in the advertising world long, but I could only imagine the amount of money Paragon spent on marketing every year.

"On a list of companies with the biggest ad budgets, they are in the top ten. We are going to San Francisco to try to convince them to hire the Bradford Agency."

"Ahh. And that would explain why the owner and CEO is going instead of anyone else?"

"Damn right. I need to let Paragon know that they are important to me and my company."

"That makes sense." Most of it. "So, what will I be doing while we're there? Won't I get in the way?"

He smiled. "Not at all. I will have plenty of stuff for you to do. Paragon's CEO is old and old-fashioned. He doesn't like PowerPoint presentations. So, whatever I decide to pitch to him will have to be printed out, and without our own resources at our fingertips, I'm going to need you to figure out where in the city we can make things happen."

Yikes. It was almost like the account would depend on how good of a job I could do. "I'll do whatever I can to help."

Seth sat back. "That's good to hear. But you don't need to worry about anything now. We're not going to get there until after eight, Pacific Time. We'll get to bed early and get a head start tomorrow morning."

"Was I that obvious about being worried?"

"Maybe a little."

The flight attendant made the announcement to put electronics in Airplane mode or to turn them off, which wasn't ideal. I wanted to start Googling for print shops in the Bay Area.

I guessed I was going to have to settle for trying to relax and not concern myself with it until tomorrow.

"What are you reading?" Seth asked, looking at my book, which was facedown in my lap.

"Um..." Normally, I wasn't embarrassed to tell people I read romance novels, but this was my boss, and this book had a particularly bold title.

"Is it that *Fifty Shades of Grey* stuff?"

I wrinkled my nose. "Hell no. I don't do billionaires." My eyes widened at the words that had flown out of my mouth on autopilot. I looked at Seth. "No offense."

Seth raised his brow.

I couldn't tell him about my history with the private school I had gone to and how the rich kids had made fun of me, so I picked the other reason I didn't like billionaire books.

"After *Fifty Shades* came out, everyone was writing billionaire books. This book was a billionaire story, this book was a billionaire story, and this book was a billionaire story. You couldn't walk two feet without tripping over one."

"You don't say?"

"It's not like I blame the authors who did this. *Fifty*

Shades was huge, and a girl's gotta eat. But it was overdone, in my opinion. Not to mention, most billionaires in real life are unattractive, old men." I side-eyed Seth. "Again, no offense."

He shrugged. "None taken. Technically, I'm a millionaire."

I snorted. "Yeah, because that's so much less money."

"Actually, it is. If you took money and turned it into time, a million seconds would be eleven and a half days. A billion seconds is almost thirty-two *years*."

My jaw dropped. "You're shitting me." I clapped my hand over my mouth. "I mean, you're kidding me."

"You can swear in front of me, Tessa. And, no, I'm not kidding."

"Wow. I had no idea there was such a difference."

"Most people don't."

"But either way, a million dollars is still much more than what most people have."

"You're very correct, which is why I try to give where I can."

A rich guy who gave back. This was interesting.

"So, where do you give money?" I asked.

"Planned Parenthood, ACLU, RAINN, Crisis Text Line, and The Trevor Project, to name a few." Seth looked away and cleared his throat. "So, if you don't read about billionaires, what kinds of guys do you read about? What does the man in your current book do for work?"

I chuckled nervously. "The hero is a stripper-slash-escort."

It was Seth's eyes that widened this time. "For real?"
"Yes, for real."
"Wow. What does the woman do?"
"The heroine is a journalist and has been sent to do an article on him."
"Hm. Is it good?"
"So far. I only just started it."
"Are you going to turn it over and show me the title?"
"Um...no."
Seth both frowned and laughed. "No?"
"No. It's not suitable for work."
He leaned in close. "We're not working, Tessa." His voice was low and sultry, and I wondered if he talked like that when he was naked and in bed with a woman.

I should have been focused on where his hand was instead of whether or not he liked to talk dirty because he snatched my book out of my lap before I could even process that he'd moved.

He stared, openmouthed, at the cover and then started to laugh.

I glared at him. "It's not funny."

I reached for my book, but he blocked me.

"I never said it was."

"Then, why are you laughing?"

"Because..." He grinned. "I don't know why. I just am. Picturing you reading a book called *Dickmatized* does something to me."

This time, when I went for my paperback, Seth let me have it.

He looked over my shoulder and said the title again, *"Dickmatized* by Leela Lou Dahlin."

I lifted my chin and met Seth's eyes. "Yes, that's the title. I personally love it."

"I like it too." He glanced down and back up at me. "So, Tessa, tell me, have you ever been dickmatized?"

Chapter Twelve

SETH

I FLIPPED to the next page of Tessa's book while she slept on my shoulder. She never answered my question on whether or not she'd ever been dickmatized, but I suspected she hadn't. She had avoided my question, but the blush on her cheeks had given her away. Which was a damn shame. This woman deserved to be dickmatized.

But I was her boss, so I didn't press the issue. I should have never asked it in the first place, but my mouth had gone off before my brain could stop it.

So, when she opened her book and stuck her nose in it, I didn't bother her anymore.

I turned on my computer and kept my mind on my own work.

But after a while, Tessa set down her book and closed her eyes. When she'd slumped over onto my shoulder, I'd closed my laptop and picked up her book.

I wasn't much of a reader, but when I did read, it

wasn't romance novels, so my curiosity was very piqued. And I had to admit, I wanted to get to the sex stuff before Tessa woke up.

But as I read it, I found that I wanted to know what was going to happen to the characters and their relationship too.

It felt like I was getting close to the good stuff when Tessa stirred and lifted her head.

I set the book down on my lap to look at her.

"Oh man." She rubbed her eyes. "How long was I out?"

"Not long. Maybe half an hour."

She laid her head back down on my shoulder and yawned. I certainly didn't mind being her pillow, but when she wrapped her arm around my bicep and pushed her breasts into me, I had to adjust the lower half of me.

I loved it when women were sexy without trying. Don't get me wrong. I liked it when they were trying, too, but there was something about them not realizing how beautiful they were that made them even more irresistible. Like Tessa was now.

If we weren't in an airplane full of people, there was a chance I would show her just how much I wanted her right now.

I lifted the book back up because if I wasn't going to be having sex, then at least I could read about someone who was.

That was probably why women read them too. I couldn't say I blamed them.

I was just getting back into the story when Tessa stiffened and lifted her head.

"Oh my God."

"What?"

"I just realized I was sleeping on you." She covered her face with her hands and slouched down in her seat. "Why am I always doing inappropriate things when it comes to you?"

I sighed. "No, you are not."

"You're my *boss*. I should not be sleeping on your shoulder."

I turned in my seat the best I could. Even in first class, I didn't have a lot of room to rotate the way I'd like to. "Okay, so how about we be friends too?"

She peeked at me through her fingers. "Go on."

I had to smile at her. "You're only working for me for twelve weeks. And, yes, I'm the one in charge, but technically, you're employed by your temp agency, not by my company. How about you and I decide right now that we're friends? You're a friend who is helping me out while my employee is out on maternity leave."

She dropped her arms and sat up. "I don't know if that actually erases the boss-employee thing, but it does make me feel a little better."

"Good, because I like you, and I think we'll be great friends."

"I know you're only humoring me, but thank you."

"Whatever you say, ol' buddy, ol' pal."

Tessa laughed. "You're a goofball."

"Thank you."

She looked down at my hands. "Is that my book?"

I picked it up and wiggled it. "It sure is."

She held out her hand. "Can I have it back?"

"Nope. We're friends now, and friends let friends borrow books."

She surprised me by plucking it right out of my hands. "You're right. But friends also ask before they borrow."

A couple of hours later, our Uber pulled up in front of our hotel. As we rolled our luggage into the lobby, Tessa yawned again.

"You're tired? But you took a nap on the plane."

"It is almost eleven o'clock our time. Nap or no nap, I am ready for bed. I've been up since six this morning."

So had I, but I was used to getting little sleep.

When we reached the counter, the gentleman standing there asked, "Checking in or checking out?"

"Checking in, please."

"Name?"

"Seth Crawford."

"One moment." He turned to his computer and started clicking away. He smiled. "I found your reservation. It looks like it's for six nights." He looked from me to Tessa. "And it's for two. Is that correct?"

"Yes."

"Sounds good." A few more clicks on the keyboard,

and a minute later, he was sliding two key cards over the counter. "Here you go."

"Which one goes to which?" I asked.

"Pardon me?"

"Which card goes to which room?" I frowned, realizing that he hadn't even said a room.

The man looked startled. "I'm sorry, sir, but there is only one room booked under your name. The presidential suite."

I turned to Tessa. "Didn't you book two rooms?"

I knew I had just said we were friends on the plane, but I wasn't sure we should share a room. More because I was attracted to her and worried I couldn't keep my hands off of her than about propriety.

She straightened. "Yes." She chewed her bottom lip and slowly closed her eyes. "Oh shit." She opened them. "No, I didn't. I was trying to do more than one thing at a time, and I think I only reserved the suite."

"It's okay," I told her. "We can ask for another room now. I'm sure it will be fine."

I turned back to the man behind the counter. By the look on his face, he was worried about something.

"I'm sorry, sir, ma'am. We have two conferences this week. We are completely booked. I thought you were taking the presidential suite because it was the only thing left."

I remembered I was wearing a T-shirt and jeans—expensive T-shirt and jeans—but they weren't a business suit. I could see why he had come to the conclusion that I had taken the suite as a last resort rather than something I had asked for.

"I know it isn't ideal, but I will just go to another hotel," Tessa said. She looked at the man. "Is there a waiting list I can get on in case something opens up?"

"No," I replied.

Tessa swung her head to me. "What?"

"No." I didn't care if we were stuck in the same room together. This proposal was too important. In fact, having her so close might help us get more work done. "I have a suite, which usually means more than one bedroom." I shot a questioning look at the man helping us.

"Two bedrooms, sir. And a pullout sofa in the main area."

"See, two bedrooms. There's no need for you to get another room at a different hotel when you can stay with me."

"Are you sure that's a good idea?"

It was one working week. We were adults. I could control my base instincts for one week, right?

Chapter Thirteen

TESSA

THE RIDE UP to our room was total silence, and I was worried Seth was mad at me. I had really messed up, and it had happened because I was texting with my friend about Seth and frosting.

The amount of guilt I felt right at that moment was eating away at me. I didn't care what he had said on the plane about being friends. Something was wrong with me when it came to Seth. I was always messing up.

We reached the hotel room, where the bellhop opened the door for us.

"Off to the left is the largest of the two bedrooms. It has an en suite bathroom. To the right is the second bedroom, and next to it is the second bathroom."

"Thank you," I said softly.

"Thank you," Seth said and pulled some money from his wallet.

"Is there anything else you need, sir?"

"No, nothing at this time."

The bellhop turned to me. "Ma'am? Is there anything I can get you?"

"No, thank you."

The bellhop nodded and left the room. The sound of the door closing behind him was deafening.

But Seth didn't seem to notice. He grabbed the handle of his suitcase and rolled it into the bigger of the two bedrooms.

Feeling overwhelmed, I took my suitcase into the other bedroom and texted Alexis.

> Me: Remember on Friday, when we were joking about frosting? Yeah, well, I messed up and forgot to book myself a room at the hotel. Now, I'm in Seth's suite—it has two bedrooms—and I'm pretty sure he's mad at me.

> Alexis: Oh no! I'm so sorry! I take the full blame for messaging you naughty stuff.

> Me: No, it's my fault. I should have waited to text you until I was done.

> Alexis: What are you going to do? Are you sure he's mad?

> Me: He seemed okay when we were checking in, but he hasn't said anything since we got up here. He went straight to his room after he tipped the bellhop.

> **Alexis:** Oh, babe. I hope everything will be okay. Maybe he just needs time to cool off.

> **Me:** I can only hope.

> **Alexis:** At least it's time for bed. He can sleep on the whole thing, realize it's not a big deal, and I'm sure he'll feel better in the morning. You will too.

> **Me:** Thank you.

Her reassurance did make me feel a little better.

> **Alexis:** Go to sleep and text me in the morning.

> **Me:** I will.

> **Alexis:** Good luck!

After saying good night to Alexis, I messaged my brother and my mom to let them know I had made it safely. Then, I snuck into the bathroom to get ready for bed.

I was hoping that the less Seth saw of me, the less annoyed he'd be about having to share a room with me.

Once I was ready for bed, I picked up the phone by my bed and dialed the front desk.

I was greeted by the same man who had checked us in. At least, I was pretty sure it was him.

"How can I help you this evening?" he asked.

"Were you the one who checked us into the presidential suite?"

"Yes." His voice was tight now.

"In all the commotion, I never did find out from you if there is a waiting list for open rooms."

"Technically, no."

"Technically?"

"But if something comes up, I would be happy to let you know."

A small sense of relief went through me. "Thank you. I'm sorry, but what is your name?"

"Doug."

"Thank you, Doug."

"It is my pleasure. Is there anything else, ma'am?"

"No. Thank you again."

I hung up the phone, feeling slightly better than when I had called. I was still stuck there tonight, but maybe tomorrow, I'd have my own room.

I opened my suitcase to find my pajamas and realized I hadn't packed anything modest to sleep in. Yes, I had my own space, but would it have killed me to include a pair of flannel pajamas in my suitcase?

It could be worse. I could have brought nothing to sleep in.

———

Seth

Despite the two-hour time difference, I couldn't sleep, and lying in bed was getting me nowhere. There was a TV in the main room, so I headed out there in hopes that watching television would get my brain to slow down so I could get some rest before tomorrow.

Before parking myself on the couch, I checked to see if the light was on in Tessa's room. I was wearing only my boxers, which I normally slept in, but I didn't want to have to put on more clothes than I needed to. I was comfortable the way I was.

When I'd agreed to share my hotel room, I hadn't considered the fact that I wouldn't be able to do everything I wanted to do when I was alone. But I was wearing about as much clothing as a man on the beach would, and since my roommate was sleeping, I figured I was fine.

I clicked through a few channels until I found reruns of a show I'd watched back when I was in college. Hopefully, it wouldn't be long before I got tired because I planned on doing a lot of work tomorrow.

It took until almost halfway through the second episode before my eyelids got heavy, so I forced myself to sit up and turn off the TV before I fell asleep on the sofa. The room went dark, except for the lights coming from the street below, and silence filled the room.

Until I heard a cry.

I stood and arched my neck to get a better sense of where the sound was coming from.

Another cry made it to my ears, and I realized it was coming from Tessa's room.

It reminded me of the day I had found her sleeping on the couch in my office. It seemed she was having a bad dream, but I didn't know if I should disturb her or not. It felt wrong to have her suffer, but it also seemed inappropriate to enter her room while she was unconscious.

But when I heard her yell, "No! *Please*," I decided if the situation were reversed, I would want someone to come and wake me up.

Just in case she wasn't sleeping, I knocked on her door. There was a whimper but nothing like a *come in* or *one moment, please*.

Still playing it safe, I slowly pushed open the door. "Tessa?"

She whimpered. "No. I don't want to. Please," she said as she thrashed her head back and forth.

I approached her bed and placed my hand on her shoulder. "Tessa. Tessa, honey, wake up."

With some gentle shaking, I was able to wake her up. The light wasn't strong in her room, but I knew that she was no longer sleeping when her body stiffened under my hand.

"Tessa, it's Seth. Are you okay?"

I figured she would tell me she was fine and to leave her alone. I wasn't prepared for her to start crying.

"I'm sorry," she said, her voice wavering.

I sat down. "Oh, Tessa, don't apologize. It's okay. We all have bad dreams." Maybe she was worried she had woken me up. "I was in the living room when I heard you. Is there anything I can do to help?"

"Can—can you hold me?"

Whoa. I had not expected that, but I completely understood that it felt good not to be alone after a nightmare.

I stood and went around to the other side of the bed. As I climbed in next to her, I reflected on the fact that I had worried about propriety when walking into her bedroom while she was sleeping. And here I was, getting into her bed.

I slid one arm under her head, and I wrapped the other around her waist, pulling her body flush with mine. "It's okay. You're safe now. Go back to sleep."

Chapter Fourteen

TESSA

I STARED at the door handle in my bedroom as if it would give me a pep talk for the courage I needed to walk out of there and face Seth.

It did no such thing.

When I had woken up this morning, I had been all alone, but that didn't help me feel less embarrassed about what had occurred in the middle of the night.

I should have known I'd have one of my nightmares after what happened with the hotel-room situation and Seth not speaking to me.

I really hated that, for some reason, I felt like people with money were better than me. I mean, that was what it boiled down to. I didn't know what it was called—internal aporophobia, I guessed—but I had it. I supposed it was no different than internalized misogyny or fatphobia, and unfortunately, being aware of it didn't magically make it go away.

But then to have Seth hear me dreaming and for me to ask him to hold me...I was mortified. I didn't care that he had obliged because he probably felt sorry for me. And since he had been gone by the time I woke up, I was guessing he had left as soon as I fell back asleep.

I could kick myself for not booking two rooms. Even though I had scheduled last minute, there were dozens of hotels in the area. I could have called around, but I'd just had to pick the one hosting two conferences this weekend.

I rolled my eyes. I didn't know how I'd gotten so lucky.

Either way, it was probably best to face Seth right now. I couldn't hide forever.

Holding my head high, I exited my bedroom.

Seth was sitting at the dining room table with his laptop open, staring intently at the screen. He was dressed in a white button-up shirt and jeans. He looked good enough to eat, but he didn't even glance up when I entered.

That wasn't a good sign.

I cleared my throat in hopes that would get his attention, but he gave no indication he'd heard me, and my heart started to race. I didn't think he was happy with me, but for him to not even look at me must mean he was really upset.

I had half a mind to quit right there, book the first flight home, and never think about this job ever again. Except I wasn't a coward. Not all of me anyway.

I pulled out the chair adjacent to Seth and sat down. With my hands folded on the table, I said, "I apologize for yesterday's events."

He blinked and turned his gaze toward me. He tilted his head to the side.

"Where would you like to go from here?" I asked. "Do you want me to find a different hotel for us to stay? One with two rooms? I can call around. Or if you changed your mind about me finding a different place, I can look for myself instead. I'm sure there is an opening nearby."

Seth stared at me for a few moments, and I started to squirm. I knew I was the one who had made the mistake, but if he thought I could read his mind, it wasn't going to happen.

I had worked at my old job for years, and while I knew the people I worked for well, I had never been able to fully anticipate what they wanted.

Seth closed his laptop.

That probably wasn't a good sign. He was probably going to fire me.

But since I had just been thinking about going back to Minnesota, getting fired wouldn't be the worst thing.

Finally, he said, "What makes you think I changed my mind?"

Ugh. I didn't want to say it out loud. *Well, see, you ignored me the whole ride up to our suite and went into your room without a word. Then, I practically begged you to sleep next to me last night because I was scared.*

I had to wonder if he got some enjoyment out of making me voice my humiliation.

I lifted a hand. "Never mind. I will make some calls

today and find somewhere else for me to stay." I pushed myself up from the chair.

"*Sit*," he commanded. His voice wasn't mean, but it was stern.

I sat.

He furrowed his brow. "What makes you think I changed my mind?" he asked again.

"Do you like torturing me?" Apparently, I was done playing nice.

"No."

I rolled my eyes. "You weren't happy last night after you agreed to let me have the second bedroom. And then I took advantage of your hospitality by asking you to comfort me last night. And just a few minutes ago, when I tried to apologize, you all but ignored me." I narrowed my eyes. "Are those reasons enough for you?"

He leaned forward. He was so close that I caught his scent. He smelled incredible, and the fire in his eyes reminded me of how good he'd felt next to me last night.

He was strong and masculine, and I had slept like a baby after he got into bed with me. I wished I could stop thinking about it.

"First of all, I was just fine last night. I don't know why you thought I wasn't happy with you, but I was thinking about the things we needed to do today. Second, you did not take advantage of me. I wanted to get in that bed with you just as much as you wanted me to. And if you had wanted more, I would have been more than willing to give it to you as well. Third, I didn't hear you apologize just now. I was concentrating on my computer because, as I said, we have a very busy day today. Fourth, you can take your apology back because I didn't ask for it and I don't want it." His brow rose. "We're friends now, remember?"

I nodded even though I didn't quite agree. What did he mean by he would have been willing to give me more? Did I even want to know?

I wasn't going to think about that right now.

"Good," he said and sat back. "Now, did you bring your computer?"

"Yes."

"Go and get it. We have work to do."

———

The rest of the day flew by. There were no more awkward conversations or any mishaps on my part. It was a normal workday, except we were in a hotel instead of at the office.

It was getting late when Seth's phone vibrated on the table, and he picked it up.

"This is Seth."

He listened for a few seconds and then grinned, but he didn't let it show in his voice when he spoke.

"I am currently in San Francisco at the moment. I can be in Los Angeles later this week. Does that work?"

Pause.

"Great. Let me hand you to my assistant to make that appointment." He put the phone on hold and smiled. "That is the head of marketing over at Functional Bean."

My eyes widened. "The coffee company run by Ryan Jackman?"

Ryan Jackman was a famous actor who had started his own coffee company.

"The one and only. Functional Bean wants to set up an appointment for me to meet with Mr. Jackman to talk about hiring us."

"Oh my God, that would be awesome. Do you think you might actually get to meet him?" I couldn't hide the excitement from my voice.

I might have a thing about rich people, but it didn't extend to celebrities. Or rather, it didn't pertain to celebrities I liked. If I met Ryan Jackman, I would probably faint from excitement. Not only was he handsome and funny, but from everything I'd ever read about him, he was down-to-earth too. If Seth got to meet him, I was going to be overcome with jealousy. And if I got to be in on that meeting, I would have to figure out a way to keep myself conscious because I wouldn't miss the opportunity for anything.

"We shall see. I need you to make an appointment to go down to Los Angeles, so we can have a meeting in person."

"What about Paragon? We don't know when we're going to meet with them yet. What if they want to meet on the same day?" That could get messy.

"There is that chance, yes, but that is the price of business. Try to set up the meeting for Thursday or Friday. If we have to change our flight, we can. If that doesn't work for them, we'll go from there."

"Got it." I took a deep breath and took the phone.

Seth chuckled. "You're not speaking to the actor himself, just the head of marketing. Relax."

He had a point.

So what that Ryan Jackman had probably hired the head of marketing? I was a professional.

I took the phone off of hold. "Good evening. This is Mr. Crawford's assistant, Tessa. I was told you'd like to set up a meeting." My voice was surprisingly calm and even.

"Yes, please," the woman on the other end said. "Mr. Jackman is out of town until Tuesday."

Perfect.

"Would Wednesday morning work for Mr. Crawford? Mr. Jackman leaves again on Thursday."

I looked at Seth and smiled apologetically since I couldn't get the meeting on the day he wanted. "Let me see. Yes, Wednesday morning is open. How does nine a.m. sound?"

"Nine a.m. it is. I will let Mr. Jackman know that Mr. Crawford will be here to see him."

"Thank you."

"Thank you."

I hit End on the phone. "Wednesday morning at nine, you are meeting with the one and only Ryan Jackman. It was all he had available. I hope that's okay."

"We'll make it work."

I folded my hands in a begging position. "Please tell me I get to be a part of this meeting. You know, to take notes and such."

Seth laughed. "Are you a fan by chance?" he teased.

"A fan? That's an understatement. I would have that man's babies if he asked."

I closed my eyes and pictured Ryan Jackman in my head. He was tall, dark, handsome, and funny.

I blew out a breath and looked at Seth, who was frowning.

"Uh-oh. Do you not like him?"

A minute ago, it'd seemed like Seth was happy to go to this meeting. Now, he looked…angry.

"I don't know. That remains to be seen. Not all actors are nice, you know."

"I know. I'm not an idiot. But from what I've read, he's a great guy."

"He's probably an asshole," Seth grumbled.

"Are you okay?"

He slammed his computer closed. "Let's go downstairs and eat. I'm tired of sitting in this room."

Chapter Fifteen

TESSA

WHEN WE GOT DOWNSTAIRS, the hotel restaurant was full, so Seth and I opted to walk out and find a restaurant. We found a casual dining place nearby. It was also busy and loud, so we spent more time eating than conversing. Or maybe that was because Seth didn't feel like talking to me. He seemed to be preoccupied, so I left him alone with his thoughts.

We walked back to the hotel in silence, and when we arrived, I knew I didn't want to go back upstairs. The only things waiting for me up there were work, sitting in more silence with my boss, or shutting myself in my room. None of those sounded appealing, so when Seth headed to the elevators, I went the opposite way.

He frowned at me. "Where are you going?"

"I'm going to head to the bar. It's not even eight yet, and I'm not ready for bed." I smiled. "This way, you can have some time alone without your last-minute roommate."

"I don't think it's wise for you to go to the bar alone."

"Thanks, but I'm twenty-eight years old. I've gone drinking by myself, and I can handle my liquor quite well. Plus, it's not like I have to drive. I just hop on the elevator, and I'm good to go." I waved. "I'll see you later."

"Tessa."

"Good-bye, Seth. Enjoy your solitude while you can."

I didn't turn back around, and he didn't call my name again, but it felt good to be by myself for a bit.

Upon entering the bar though, I realized it was going to be harder to stay by myself than I'd thought. I had planned to get a table in the corner, sip on a glass of wine, and read my book that I had tucked into my purse. But all the tables were full, so I picked a spot at the bar.

After giving the bartender my order, I sat back in my stool and looked around. Most people there were in large groups, and I concluded that most of them were part of the conferences the hotel was hosting. They had probably finished for the day and escaped for a drink.

I could relate.

The bartender brought me my wine, but rather than pull my book out, I chose to look through my social media. To be honest, I didn't want anyone making fun of me for reading at the bar. But I hoped I could scroll on my cell for a bit, and then maybe I'd get lucky and get a table soon.

I went to Instagram first but got bored and went over to Facebook. I was a member of various reader groups, and it had been a few days since I'd checked in. I got some of the best book suggestions from these groups.

As I read through some posts, I found quite a few books I wanted to read, and I commented on others where people asked for recommendations.

Someone brushed my arm as they sat down on the stool next to me. I looked up to see an older but very handsome gentleman. His dark hair was silver on the edges, but it only made him more striking.

I quickly looked away before he caught me staring and went back to my phone.

Thankfully, I found a story that had me laughing, and I momentarily forgot about the man next to me.

"If it's not too much trouble, I'd love to hear what is so funny."

I lifted my head and glanced around. I pointed to my chest. "Me?"

The gentleman smiled. "Yes, you. I heard you laughing, and it's been a long day. I could use a laugh."

"Okay, but if I repeat it, it's not going to be funny. I'm not a good storyteller."

He motioned with his hand. "Let me read it for myself then."

"Are you going to steal my phone?" I asked coyly.

He looked down at his very expensive suit and back up at me. "Maybe. Not because I need it, but because today was very boring, and I could use some entertainment."

This made me smile, and I pushed my phone over to him. "Have at it."

He picked up my cell, and I sipped my wine while he

read. Soon, he was laughing out loud, and then he pushed my mobile back over to me.

"Good story, huh?"

"It was exactly what I needed." He lifted his glass to me. "Thank you."

"You're welcome."

"Are you here for business or pleasure?" he asked me.

"Business. I take it, you are too?"

"Yes. But it would be much better if it were for pleasure," he said, meeting my eyes.

I blushed and turned away.

The man was very handsome, but for some reason, my mind immediately went to Seth, and I felt like I was betraying him.

It was such a bizarre thought.

I had come to the conclusion that I liked Seth, and he wasn't like some of the other stuck-up rich people I knew, but I also realized that I had a little bit of a crush on him, which was inconvenient. Seth was my boss, and even if he wasn't, he was way out of my league.

This man was out of my league, too, but the difference was, we both knew it would be a one-night stand with a stranger who lived in a different town and probably a different state. He didn't have to worry about what his social circle would think of me. And I didn't have to worry about impressing him or keeping up with him either. It would only be about sex.

I knew I'd said I didn't like rich people, but a few hours of pleasure wouldn't hurt me, would it?

I held out my palm. "I'm Tessa," I said.

He shook my hand and squeezed. "I'm Gregory."

Seth

I paced back and forth in my hotel room.

When I had gotten upstairs after dinner, I had tried to work some more. That wasn't even remotely successful.

I had also tried to watch TV and even called my mom and then my brother, Dex, to see how my nephew was doing. I was desperate, yet nothing was working to keep my mind off of Tessa.

Finally, I couldn't take it anymore, and I went looking for her.

All day, I had been thinking about how good she had felt against me last night and how much I'd liked waking up with her in my arms.

I had liked it too much because I woke up with a painful erection that refused to go away. My stupid dick would not let me enjoy lying in bed with Tessa. It was too busy, thinking about being inside her, to the point that it was all I could think about after a while. Eventually, I gave up and left her bed.

I had tried to go back to sleep in my own room, but I'd been too horny, so I had gotten up for the day and started some work.

So, going downstairs to the bar while I was running

low on sleep wasn't the best idea I'd had, but I didn't care. I wanted to know what Tessa was doing. I was still irritated with her for telling me that she wanted to have Ryan Jackman's babies. It wasn't like he was here in our hotel, but it bothered me enough that I wanted to check on her.

The bar was crowded when I got there, and I couldn't find her right away. There were two elevators, and I considered that maybe she had gone upstairs on one while I had come down on the other. But then a small group of people parted, and there she was, sitting at the bar.

And she wasn't alone.

I gritted my teeth and headed right for her.

I was already fuming before I reached her, but when she arched her beautiful neck and laughed at whatever the guy had said, I was pissed. To make matters worse, he put his hand on top of hers, and she didn't pull away.

Only from years of putting up a good front while working with asshole clients was I able to pull myself together when I reached her.

"Tessa," I said with a smile to show that I came in peace. I put my hand on the small of her back and slid it up to the back of her neck to show the man with her that she wasn't to be messed with.

He quickly snatched his hand away.

His back straightened. "I'm sorry. Tessa didn't tell me she was here with anyone."

I gave him a hard smile. "Well, she is."

Tessa's eyes darted back and forth between the two of us. "Gregory, you don't understand," she said.

He smiled politely at her, threw some bills on the bar, and said, "You don't have to explain." He nodded to the two of us. "I hope you have a good night."

I dropped down in Gregory's now-empty seat, where Tessa shot visual daggers at me.

"What did you do that for?"

I scoffed. "You know he only wanted to fuck you, right?"

I expected her to balk or gasp or be horrified.

She completely blindsided me when she said, "Yeah, Seth, I know. Why do you think I was talking to him?"

Because I hadn't been prepared for her response, my own burst out of me before I could stop it.

I got in her face and growled, "The only person who's going to be fucking you tonight or any other day this week is me."

This time, I got the initial reaction I had expected.

Her eyes rounded, and she sucked in a breath. "Bullshit," she whispered.

I made a single nod toward her wineglass. "How many of those have you had to drink?"

Her eyes didn't leave my face. "This is my first one."

And it was only about half-empty.

This time, it was me who stood and threw bills on the bar top. But instead of saying good-bye, I grabbed her hand and led her back upstairs.

Chapter Sixteen
TESSA

SETH PULLED me into the elevator behind him, determination in his whole body. He didn't let go of my hand as he turned us around to face the front, and I gave an experimental tug to see if he'd let go.

He didn't budge.

And when another couple started walking toward us, Seth hit the Close Door button and barked out, "Get the next one."

The couple was too startled to argue, and seconds later, it was the two of us, alone.

I turned to him to ask him what had gotten into him when he pushed me against the wall and took my mouth.

His free hand cupped my face as his lips landed on mine. Within seconds, he urged my mouth open and slid his tongue inside.

I was pretty sure no one's boss was supposed to taste this good.

He kissed his way down my cheek and sucked on my neck, pushing his hard length against me.

I gasped, digging my hands into his sides and rubbing my cleft against him. "Oh God," I muttered.

Foreplay with one's boss definitely shouldn't feel this good.

I was so into Seth's actions that I barely noticed the doors to the elevator opening until he pulled away from me and took my hand again.

When we reached our suite, he already had his key card out and opened the door within seconds. He tugged me inside and pushed me against the wall to kiss me again. My purse slid off my shoulder and landed with a *thunk* by our feet.

He lifted his head to meet my eyes. "Unless you tell me no, I'm going to take you into my room and fuck you so good. But only if you want to."

I licked my bottom lip. "Yes."

Groaning, he swiped his thumb over my wet lip and then grasped the front of my neck. "I can't wait to take you," he said against my mouth and dropped to his knees.

I shivered. I couldn't wait either.

He unbuttoned the front of my pants and pulled one leg out of my underwear and pant leg. He kissed the side of my thigh and looked up. As he stared into my eyes, he put his mouth on my cleft and licked my clit.

His tongue was hot and gentle at first. I clutched at the wall with one hand and his hair with the other, but soon, I was rubbing my crotch on his face.

There was a moment of clarity that I was going to be embarrassed about this tomorrow, but right now, I was chasing an orgasm and didn't give a single damn.

I shouldn't be surprised that Seth was a master at giving head, but I was surprised when he stood up before I could come.

"What did I ever do to you?" I whined.

He chuckled and kissed me. "You've been driving me crazy since the moment you walked up to me and demanded who I was. And as a reward to myself for keeping my hands off you this long, you're not coming until I'm inside you."

He slid his hands under my butt, picked me up, and carried me to the bedroom. As he laid me on the bed, he was already pulling off the other leg of my pants. He pushed my legs up and out and rubbed his fingers on me.

I flinched. "If you're not going to finish, stop teasing."

He smiled and pushed two fingers into me.

A low moan escaped me.

"Not teasing. I just wanted to check how ready you were for me."

"Very ready."

"That's what they all say."

I thought he was making a joke about all the women wanting him until he stripped off his shirt and unzipped his pants. He pushed his boxers and jeans off his hips, and the most impressive cock I'd ever seen sprang out and slapped him on the stomach. It almost touched his belly button.

"Holy shit," I whispered.

"Now, you understand why I need you ready," he said matter-of-factly and not cocky at all. His confidence without the arrogance was sexy as hell.

I tugged on the bottom of my shirt to pull it off. "Please tell me you have a condom." To wait this long and not get to have Seth inside me would be the worst thing about the whole trip.

My shirt made it over my head, and I flung it aside as a row of condoms landed on the bed beside me.

My eyes widened. "Are all those for me?"

He smirked. "Maybe. I guess we'll see how much you want it."

"Oh, I want it."

"As much as you wanted Gregory?"

I licked my lips. "More. Much more. The only reason Gregory was in the picture was because I didn't think I had a chance with you."

Seth ran his hands down the inside of my legs and brushed his thumbs over my mound. "Why would you think that?"

"I don't know. Just because."

He pushed one thumb against my clit but didn't move. "That's not true. I know you know."

He circled my bundle of nerves but only once, and I whimpered.

"Tell me, and you get more."

It was hard to think when I was so turned on, but I

picked the most obvious reason and hoped he accepted my answer.

"Okay, well, how about you're my boss and I'm your employee?"

Circle...circle...circle.

"I thought we already talked about this on the plane. I don't actually employ you. There's more."

I shook my head.

He pushed his other thumb inside me. "Don't lie, Tessa."

This man could teach classes in torture.

"As if you don't know that you're hot and rich and nice, I mean, let's not forget Amy."

He gave me some more stimulation, playing me like I was a piano and he was Beethoven. "Thank you for the compliment, but what does that have to do with you?"

"I'm none of those things," I admitted. "Except nice but only when I want to be. I'm not even close to being rich, and while I know I'm pretty, I'm not nearly as hot as you."

"There, that wasn't so hard," he said.

I was prepared for him to step away from me and go for the condoms, but he didn't stop touching me. He withdrew his thumb and pushed two fingers into my pussy as he continued to rub my clit.

I gripped the bedding underneath me as my breathing both quickened and shallowed. I was so close, but I held off, remembering what he'd said. Stopping mid-orgasm was worse than not having one at all.

He must have sensed my hesitation. "Come, Tessa. It's okay. I got you."

I let go, and as soon as my climax hit, Seth pulled his hand from inside me and drove his cock in there instead.

My already-strong orgasm hit me even harder as he stretched my walls. My back arched off the bed, and I thought I might pass out from lack of air. But I didn't care because I was floating on the best pleasure high ever.

"Perfection," Seth said, cupping my breasts and thumbing my nipples as my senses returned.

He slid his cock from my body and went for a condom.

"Roll over," he said, and I slowly got onto my hands and knees.

I heard the tearing of the wrapper and a sigh as he put the rubber on.

I wiggled my ass to let him know I was ready. Orgasm or not, I wanted to feel him pound his beautiful dick in me.

He gripped my hips and groaned. "I love these."

"You do?" I knew some men liked big hips and big butts. I just hadn't thought Seth would be one of them.

"Fuck yes," he said and thrust inside me.

"Oh God." I dropped down onto my chest, so my ass was in the air and so Seth's dick would hit me—

Yes, right there.

He felt amazing in me, and stroke after stroke after stroke built me up until I felt like I could come again. I shoved my hand between my legs to touch myself and went straight for my swollen nub. I tapped my fingers against it to match Seth's rhythm.

The stimulation did the trick, and I exploded again, but this time, I took Seth with me.

I was lying with my face still half-planted in the mattress, enjoying my post-coital bliss when he smacked my ass.

My pussy clenched around him, and my mouth dropped open. "Holy shit, what was that for?" It wasn't too painful, just a little sting. But it had been very unexpected.

"For thinking you're not good enough for me." *Smack*. "And that's for thinking you're not good enough for anyone."

"It's not my fault. It's the world we live in."

Seth pulled out and shuffled into the bathroom, where I assumed he was disposing of the condom.

I rolled onto my side, and he lay down beside me.

"Ignore them. Society doesn't speak for everyone," he said as he ran his hands over me.

"I know." Even though I wasn't small or skinny, I'd had plenty of men want me in my adult life. "It's just that you're kind of society with your money and all."

He pulled me against him. "That's where you're wrong. I'm not society. I'm me." His cock grew hard against my stomach. "And I want you. I guess I'll have to show you how much."

Chapter Seventeen
TESSA

I BLINKED up at the ceiling. Just after four in the morning, according to the clock on the nightstand, and something had woken me. The good news was, it wasn't a bad dream. The bad news was, I thought my brain had processed last night, and now, I was fully aware that I'd been sleeping in my boss's bed.

Putting my hand over my eyes, I stifled a groan. Last night felt so surreal. Almost like it hadn't happened or that it'd happened in a movie, except for the very naked man sleeping next to me.

I couldn't quite believe we'd had sex.

The best, most excellent sex—he was better in bed than I'd ever imagined he'd be—but sex nonetheless.

And now, I didn't know what to do.

The careless, *throw caution to the wind* woman I had been last night was still sleeping. And the *consequences of my actions* woman was wide awake, and she was worried that she had messed up her job. Even though Seth had reminded me that I wasn't technically his employee, he might feel differently this morning.

But I wasn't going to get anything figured out if I stayed in his bed. So, I gently slipped out from under the covers and tiptoed out of the room after picking up my clothes. I made a quick stop in the entryway to pick up my purse and headed for my own room.

When I got there, I crawled into my bed because it was still early. But that didn't stop me from grabbing my phone, so I could text Alexis.

> Me: Are you sitting down?

I knew she was still sleeping, so I didn't wait for her answer.

> Me: I had sex last night.

> Me: With Seth.

> Me: Call me ASAP because I'm freaking out!

I forced myself to set my cell on the nightstand because my friend probably wouldn't be up for a couple more hours, and constantly checking it wouldn't make her respond any faster.

But knowing I wasn't going to fall back asleep without some assistance, I also pulled my book from my purse, so I could read. Maybe inserting myself in someone else's situation, even if fictional, would stop me from thinking about what I had done last night.

Thankfully, I was a book lover because I was able to get into my story after a few pages. I read only a few chapters before my eyelids felt heavy, but now, I didn't want to stop because I was getting closer to the best part in the book.

But even the promise of reading sexy scenes couldn't stop sleep from trying to take over. I set my open book down on my chest and told myself, *Just ten minutes.*

I didn't know how long I had actually been out because I woke up to Seth pushing my door open. He scratched his head, and his eyes were barely open.

"There you are," he said with a smile and flung something on my lap before getting into bed with me. He stuck out his chin in a fake pout. "Why'd you leave me?"

I laughed, having never seen this side of him before. He was adorably cute, which only made him sexier to me.

But I couldn't tell him I'd panicked this morning, so I lifted my book for him to see. "I couldn't sleep, so I came in here to read."

He snatched the book out of my hand and tossed it over his shoulder. "You don't need that anymore. I'm here now."

I was already getting wet for him, but I needed to make something clear first. "Listen, that is not how we treat books. If there is so much as a corner bent, I'm coming after you."

Seth looked at me with heat in his eyes and picked up the item he'd thrown on my lap. "Why don't you put this on me? That way, I can make it up to you."

I slid my hand under the covers and wrapped it around his cock. He was already hard, and I loved it.

"You think giving me some D is going to make up for my book?" I teased.

He cocked an eyebrow. "How about *a lot* of D? Because after last night, I want to give you so much more."

I stroked him but also looked away, as if to consider his offer.

But before I could form a good response, he said, "How about a lot of D and ten new books?"

I chuckled, looking back at him. "Wow, you must really want the P."

"If it's your P, the answer is always yes."

I knew it was all pillow talk, and we'd only slept with each other one night, but his words made me feel special and sexy.

I snatched the condom from him. "You've got yourself a deal."

I awoke sometime later to my phone beeping multiple times. I was alone, and the sun was shining through my windows.

I picked up my cell to see that Alexis had messaged me back.

> Alexis: Oh my fucking God.

> Alexis: Was it good? Please tell me it was good.

> Alexis: And let me know when you're alone, so I know it's safe to call.

Rather than text her back, I just called her.

"Tessa Archer, you naughty, naughty minx."

I laughed. "Guilty."

"So, was it good?"

"What do you think?"

"I think it rocked your world."

I laughed at the old phrase we used to say in high school. "Yes. Yes, it was."

"Where is he now?"

"I don't know. Probably getting ready for the day or something like that."

"I want to hear all the details."

"Hold on." I got out of bed, opened my door, and peeked around it to see if Seth was out there. I didn't hear anything, so I figured I'd guessed right about him being in his room. "Okay, here's what happened…"

When I was done with my story, Alexis said, "Wow. That's so hot. I need to get some dick. I have only had sex with one guy since my divorce, and it was barely worth the time it had taken to put on the condom."

"I'm sorry, babe. Maybe we should go out when I get back. Find you a man…for a night," I quickly added.

"Sigh. That means I have to wait until you get back," Alexis said, and I laughed. "Until then, I'm going to live vicariously through you."

"I'll keep you updated. We do have three more nights here."

Alexis clicked her tongue. "I knew I should have sent lemon frosting with you."

Chapter Eighteen
SETH

I CLOSED MY COMPUTER. "Let's go somewhere for lunch."

Tessa looked up from her own computer. "Okay. Where are you thinking?"

Anywhere that's not this hotel room.

I was finding it hard to resist her and not take her to bed again. She was hotter than I had imagined she would be. So responsive. It made me hard, just thinking about it.

But Paragon had called that morning, and we had set up a dinner meeting. It was more of a meet and greet, but I wanted to be as prepared as possible in case they suddenly said something like, *Let's go back to the office, and you can show us your proposal.* As much as I wanted to pull Tessa into my bedroom, I knew we had to wait.

"I'm not sure. Let's go out and take another walk. We passed a lot of restaurants last night. Maybe they'll be less crowded today."

Tessa shut the lid on her laptop. "Sounds good to me."

We didn't have to go far when we found a cute little bistro.

Once we ordered our food, I asked a question that had been on my mind, "How did you end up taking this assistant job?"

Tessa sucked on the straw in her drink. "What do you mean?"

"You and your friend have this business plan, but here you are, working for me."

She sighed. "It's kind of a long story."

I gestured to our table. "We have time."

She smiled. "It seems we do."

"I'm all ears."

"Alexis used to be married, and her husband was an asshole. He bullied her into quitting her job because he wanted her to be a stay-at-home wife and mother. Those are my words, not hers. At the time, she claimed she was perfectly happy to stay home, but I think part of that was because she thought they'd have kids right away. For the record, they were married four years and didn't have any children."

"Ah." I could already see where this would cause a problem.

"Her ex refused to get tested for anything and blamed not getting pregnant on Alexis even though her doctor said they couldn't find anything medically that would prevent her from having children. Except maybe stress, but who knows for sure when her ex wouldn't get checked? Anyway, to pass the time, Alexis started baking. She'd always been good at it, but she began coming up with her own recipes, and they were really delicious."

"I can confirm that. I still have dreams about that lemon cupcake."

Tessa gave me a *you're not funny* look. "I guess I can't blame you for loving the cupcake that was supposed to be for *me*.

"Anyway, after Alexis's divorce, she went back to work. Actually, she went back to work after they separated, but that's not important. The thing was, with a full-time job, she realized how much she missed baking. Of course, I—and the rest of our friends—missed getting to eat her desserts." Tessa smiled. "One day, I said she should open her own bakery. I was half-joking. You know, one of those things. And she said, 'Let's do it.' I never went to college, and I had a good job, but I didn't love it, so I figured, why the hell not?"

I smiled. I loved hearing her tell this story.

"Fast-forward about a year. Alexis got her divorce. We hadn't wanted to do anything with our idea until that was finalized."

I nodded. "Smart."

"We started planning. We found a strip mall being built. We both knew it would be a perfect location, so we kicked our plans into high gear. I put in my six-month notice at my job. They had been good to me, so I wanted to make sure I could train the person who came after me.

Plus, I knew I had time with the mall still being under construction."

As a boss, I appreciated how good Tessa had been to her previous employer.

"The strip mall is almost completed now, and Alexis and I were planning to put a down payment on the location, but we ran into a money issue. Alexis's ex-husband comes from some money—they're not as rich as you—and when they were married, he had enough to buy a large house for him and Alexis. Now that they're divorced, he's supposed to sell the house and give Alexis half the proceeds, but so far, he has refused to sell it. He claims that she never made any payments, but he already agreed to it when they got divorced. Also, she would have contributed money if he hadn't forced her to quit her job."

"What a dick."

She snorted. "Tell me about it."

"So, this money was intended to go toward the building?" I asked.

"Yes. And since we don't have all the funds yet to get the mortgage and I already left my job, I went to a temp agency." She held out her hands. "And now, here I am."

"That sucks."

"It does, but I have hope. I know you started out with a business partner. How did you two get your business off the ground?"

I cleared my throat. I didn't like talking about John, but she wasn't really asking about him specifically. "We worked for another agency, and our boss was a real prick.

When we started our company, some of the clientele followed us. And we were able to work from home for a while."

"Yeah, working from home isn't really an option with a bakery and café."

I chuckled. "Not really."

"So, was it hard to start on your own?"

I shrugged. "Sure, but it's worth it. Now, show me the location of the strip mall."

I felt bad for cutting Tessa off from further discussion about how I'd started my own business, but I didn't want to talk or think about those days anymore. They were bittersweet, and I couldn't go back there.

Thankfully, she didn't seem to mind. She picked up her phone. "I have pictures."

After lunch, we walked back to the hotel a different way and happened to come upon a bakery.

I stopped and pointed to it. "Look at that."

"Let's go in and look around. Maybe I'll get some ideas."

"Also, a little dessert never hurt anyone. Maybe they'll have lemon cupcakes."

Tessa smiled and shook her head at me before going in.

We just got in the door when she stopped suddenly and gasped.

"What?" I asked.

"It's a cat café."

"Is that a good thing or a bad thing?" I honestly couldn't tell.

"It's a good thing. But I'm super jealous."

"You haven't opened your business yet. You can still decide to do a cat café."

Her mouth dropped open just as an employee came over to greet us.

"Hello. Is there anything I can help you with?"

"We came in for dessert, and someone has cat-café envy."

The woman smiled. "Do you like cats?"

"Love them. I have two."

"You do?" I asked.

"I do."

"What are their names?" the woman asked.

"Persephone and Hades."

"I like it," the woman said. She held out her hand. "Why don't you have a look around? Please, let me know if you need anything."

"Will do," I told her.

The woman walked away.

"Let's go check out the desserts."

"Okay." Tessa chewed on her lip as we made our way over to the bakery case. "Do you really think I could do a cat café?"

"I don't see why not. You should okay it with Alexis first though. And you'd probably have to check with zoning laws, but I'm sure you could figure it out."

I could practically see the wheels turning in her head, and I grinned.

We stopped at the counter, and I took a look at the bakery case while Tessa was perusing the shelf next to it that displayed items for sale.

She pulled something off. "Oh my God, I have to get this."

She turned and showed it to me. It was a mug that said *My Bookshelf Is My Boyfriend*.

"Cute," I said.

"It's more than cute. It's funny. Not only do I like to read, but this also reminds me of my friends."

"How so?"

She smiled to herself. "Oh, just a little club we have."

"A club?" I asked.

But she didn't seem to get that I was fishing for more information because she said, "Yep," and then she pointed to the bakery case. "Look, lemon cupcakes."

"How many should we get?" I asked.

"That depends on how many you want to eat. But I wouldn't mind getting a dozen," she said.

"A dozen should last us until we go home."

"I wonder if we can buy some extra frosting on the side."

"Huh?"

Tessa laughed. "Never mind. It's kind of a joke."

I furrowed my brow. "I need to hear this joke about frosting. Is it dirty?"

"Seriously, it's nothing," Tessa said as she turned to pay.

"Come on. I have a good sense of humor."

"Nope. It's an inside joke. You wouldn't understand," Tessa insisted.

"Maybe you can explain it to me later." I could only hope.

Chapter Nineteen

SETH

TESSA and I had worked the rest of the afternoon and were now on the way to the restaurant to meet with Paragon.

"Are you nervous?" she asked.

"Some."

"Just some?"

"I've been doing this awhile now. When I first started, I would break out in a sweat every time we met with a new client, but I've gotten somewhat used to it."

"But even though this is a huge company that could bring in thousands of dollars, you're not nervous?"

I grinned at her. "That's where the *some* comes in."

"I wish I had your nerves of steel."

Our Uber pulled up to the restaurant, and Tessa and I got out.

"What's the plan again if they spring a meeting on us at the last minute?" I asked.

"You're going to go with them to their office while I run back to the hotel and grab your laptop and the presentation, and I'll meet you there," Tessa answered.

Earlier, I'd had a Zoom meeting with the rest of our creative crew back in the office, working on the Paragon proposal, and we'd finalized the ad we wanted to present to them. Our design team had finished off the rest of it, and Tessa had gone to pick up a rush order of some big cardboard cutouts we could use to show the CEO how serious we were.

"I think we're ready. Let's head inside."

The hostess greeted us.

"We're meeting the Ainsworth party," I said.

She pulled out two menus. "Right this way, please."

When we reached the table, a gentleman stood. Old enough to be my father and then some, he had a full head of hair, but it was completely white, except for a few strands of gray here and there.

I held out my hand. "Seth Crawford."

He took it. "Gene Ainsworth," he said. "And this is my daughter, Gwyneth."

Gwyneth held out her hand, so I shook it. She was fair and blonde and younger than me.

I had done my research on the Ainsworths, and Gwyneth was the daughter from Gene's third marriage. He also had two daughters from his first marriage and a son from his second. The other daughters didn't have much to do with the company, and the son had been in and out of drug rehab since his teens.

"This is my assistant, Tessa Archer."

"Please sit," Mr. Ainsworth said.

I sat across from him while Tessa sat across from the daughter.

"Thank you for coming all this way," Gwyneth said.

"It's our pleasure," I told her. "San Francisco is a beautiful city, and I can always use an excuse to visit."

Gene turned to Tessa and looked her up and down. "What about you, dear?"

Tessa looked uncomfortable, and to be fair, there was something about the way Gene had addressed her that rubbed me the wrong way.

"This is my first time here," she said.

"Well, welcome to our city." He smiled. Or at least, it was supposed to be a smile. It came off as more of a leer.

"Thank you," she said, but she seemed anything but thankful. Her body was stiff, and she almost looked pained.

I hoped she was okay.

Tessa

I didn't like Gene Ainsworth. He made me think of a dirty old man, and I didn't trust him. Whenever Seth's attention was elsewhere, Gene would look at me with creepy lust in his eyes. The worst part was, he might have hidden it from Seth, but he made no qualms about letting his daughter see it, and I could tell it made her uncomfortable.

Dinner seemed to last forever. Before the night had started, I had been worried the man would want to see Seth's proposal, and I would have to scramble to get everything from the hotel. But by the end, I was praying he'd ask for it, so I could have an excuse to leave.

Unfortunately for me, he kept the evening all about dinner and small talk.

I did get a break when Seth's phone buzzed on the table between our plates. It was the same number that had called yesterday for Ryan Jackman. Since it was after working hours and Seth had a meeting with Mr. Jackman tomorrow morning, I figured it was important and I should answer it.

"Excuse me," I said, picking up the cell and exiting the table for a quieter spot. "Seth Crawford's phone. How may I help you?" I answered.

"Hello. I believe you are the person I spoke to yesterday to set a meeting," the woman on the other line said.

"Yes, this is his assistant."

"I am very sorry, but Mr. Jackman will not be able to make it tomorrow in person. Is there any way that Mr. Crawford can do the meeting over the phone at the same time? He'll be driving, so he can't do a Zoom meeting either."

I honestly didn't know how Seth would feel about that, but I assumed that he would rather do a phone meeting than no meeting at all since I wasn't being offered an alternative time.

"Yes, a phone meeting will be fine."

"This number?"

"Yes, please."

"Thank you for your assistance."

"Thank you."

I hit End and returned to the table. Seth looked at me, so I smiled to let him know everything was okay.

When we were finally finished with our meal, Mr. Ainsworth brought up when we would meet again. "Seth, I like what I'm hearing. I would like to set up a meeting with you at our office. You can meet the others and maybe show us what you have to offer. Does that work for you?"

Seth beamed, and I was happy for him. Despite how gross Mr. Ainsworth seemed, he hadn't done anything more than look at me. And since he lived in California and I lived in Minnesota, I hoped that after this week, I'd never have to see him again.

"That sounds great," Seth said.

"How does Thursday sound?" Mr. Ainsworth said. "We are meeting with another agency from Washington tomorrow."

This guy was an asshole. He hadn't needed to bring that up. He only wanted Seth to know he had competition. I wanted to blurt out that Seth had a meeting with Ryan Jackman tomorrow, so we couldn't have done it anyway.

But that choice was up to Seth, and he didn't say a word.

"Thursday works for us."

Mr. Ainsworth smiled, but it was a look that said his

suggestion had better work for us or else we'd lose out. I turned away, so I could roll my eyes. He was so full of himself. He was the kind of rich person I had disliked all my life. He had money, and he abused his power with it.

"What time works best?" Seth asked.

Crap. I should have probably been the one to ask that.

I quickly lifted my phone and pretended to check the calendar. "Sorry. Yes, what time would you like us there?"

"Can you come at two in the afternoon?" Gwyneth asked.

I paused a minute before saying, "We can make that work."

Gwyneth's smile was genuine, but Gene's was slightly strained.

"We shall see you then," he said. He directed his eyes at me. "And, Tessa, if you'd like some company while you're sightseeing, please just let me know."

Gross.

I wanted to lean into Seth for comfort, but he wasn't my boyfriend, and it would look very bad for me to do that to my boss.

"Thanks," I muttered through my revulsion.

We said good-bye to the father-daughter pair and went outside to wait for our Uber.

Seth scanned the area behind us before asking, "What do you think that was about?"

"Which part?" I asked dryly. It was good to know Seth wasn't completely clueless.

"Gene Ainsworth offering to take you sightseeing." He shuddered. "It was kind of creepy."

Here was where I had to make a decision. Seth and his company could make a lot of money with Paragon, and I was only going to be with the company for a few months. I didn't want to leave Seth with a bad taste in his mouth because of me.

So, I opted to play it off.

I laughed awkwardly. "He's old, and his generation thinks they're being polite, but I think they forget that women are more independent than they were in their day."

Seth studied me. "If you say so. It still rubbed me the wrong way."

I waved off his concern. "Just think of all the dollar signs that are coming your way."

He frowned and turned toward me. He was about to say something when his phone beeped to let us know our ride was approaching.

I hoped that meant we were done with this conversation because I really hated lying to him even if it was for his own good and only by omission. Thankfully, I had other news to deliver.

"Ryan Jackman can't make the meeting tomorrow, so you're going to do it over the phone. I hope that's okay. I wasn't really given a choice."

"No, that works great. We don't have to get up early to drive down to LA. But I bet you're bummed about not meeting him, right?"

I sighed. "I guess my dreams of him falling in love with me and whisking me off to marry him are over," I joked.

Seth put his arm around my neck and pressed his mouth near my ear. "Is it wrong that hearing you talk like that makes me jealous?"

Butterflies fluttered in my stomach. "No, not at all."

Chapter Twenty

TESSA

WHEN WE GOT BACK to the hotel, I was still feeling uneasy, and since I didn't want to talk about Gene Ainsworth anymore, I went to my room to change into my pajamas.

I was about to head to the bathroom to brush my teeth and wash my face when the bag from the cat café caught my eye. I hadn't brought up the idea to Alexis yet, but I could definitely share the mug with my friends.

I took a picture, making sure they could read the *My Bookshelf Is My Boyfriend* on the side, and sent it to our message group.

> Me: Look what I found. I thought it was perfect, considering I'm a founding member of United She-Woman Single Ladies with Our Vibrators So We Never Have Another Bad Date or Experience Romance Again Because Men Suck Club.

> Pru: LOL. That is perfect.

> Bree: I agree.

> Alexis: Except she might not need her bookshelf anymore.

> Bree: What does that mean?

I sighed. Alexis had done so well until now.

> Alexis: When you Googled Tessa's new boss, you forgot to look at pictures of him.

I needed to stop this before it got too far.

> Me: When Alexis came to work and brought me cupcakes, she met my boss.

> Alexis: Yeah, and he's hot.

I opened up a message thread that went to just Alexis.

> Me: You promised you wouldn't say anything. Do not tell them I had sex with Seth!

I set my phone down to wrap my mug back up in the paper, so it would be safe in my suitcase when I traveled back home, and my phone started beeping nonstop.

I unlocked the screen and cursed.

> Pru: You had sex with your boss?!
>
> Bree: Oh my God! That's so not like you!
>
> Paisley: I'm just catching up, but I agree!
>
> Isabelle: I just got here, too, but you go, girl.
>
> Elizabeth: Same here. I agree with Isabelle.

I fell back on my bed and groaned. I had opened the other message thread with Alexis but accidentally clicked back to the group one and just told everyone I'd had sex with Seth.

> Bree: Tessa, are you still there?

> Paisley: Damn, girl. I just looked up your boss. Holy hell, he is hot. I'm so jealous you're getting some and not me. P.S. Cool mug, btw.

Paisley was the queen of one-night stands, but she also had a habit of falling in love. So, while the rest of us had decided to give up dating, Paisley had pretty much had to include sex too.

> Alexis: I would just like to note that all I said was, your boss was hot. You told everyone you had sex with him.

She didn't have to include my name. I knew she was talking to me.

> Me: I know it was all me. But since I already said something, all I can say is, don't judge me. He's hot and nice. And I'm kind of on vacation.

> Paisley: You don't have to justify getting laid to me.

> Me: Thank you.

> Paisley: I am a little irked you only told Alexis and not me though.

> Pru: Yeah, what Paisley said.

Bree: I agree. I mean, I'm going to be your future sister-in-law.

Me: I thought you and Zack weren't talking about marriage?

Bree: Don't turn this around on me, young lady.

Me: LOL. You'll just have to wait until our next dinner together to get any juicy details.

Bree: Fine. It is getting late anyway.

Paisley: I will try to make time.

Pru: Me too.

Isabelle: Me three.

Elizabeth: I'll make time too.

Me: Sounds good. When I get back, we'll talk.

Me: I love you all. And have a good night.

Despite exposing myself to my friends, I had a big smile on my face after saying good night. I really loved all of them and was lucky to have them in my life. Not everyone stayed close with their high school friends.

My phone rang, and I saw it was Bree video-calling me.

I rolled onto my stomach, moved to the center of the bed to get more comfortable, and answered. "Yes?" I said in way of a greeting.

I could see that Bree was in bed, lying on her side with the covers tucked under her arms. The light was low, and I remembered she was two hours later than me. The sun was going down here in California, which meant it was already dark there.

"Crap, I completely forgot about the time change when I texted you all. I can't believe you're still awake."

"It's just after ten, not three in the morning."

"On a work night," I added.

"I'm in bed already."

"I see that. What's up?"

"You know why I'm calling. You're on my shit list."

"I'm sorry, okay? I wouldn't have even told Alexis, but she came to my work. And I've been trying to resist him. Trust me."

"Trying to resist who?" a deep voice asked behind me.

I looked over my shoulder to see a half-naked Seth before he crawled on top of me. He pushed my hair off one shoulder and kissed my neck.

"Oh my God, is that him?"

Seth lifted his head, and his body stiffened. "I didn't know you were on video," he whispered to me.

"Sorry," I whispered back.

"Hello," he said to Bree.

But before she could say hi back, my brother popped up from behind Bree. He was also naked from the waist up. At least, I hoped he was, except he was in bed with my friend so he was probably completely nude. I absolutely did not want to think about that.

"Who the fuck is that?" Zack asked.

Seth stiffened again, but I could tell it was for a different reason.

"Seth, this is my friend Bree and my brother, Zack. Guys, this is Seth."

Bree looked over at my brother and said something that I couldn't make out.

"Yeah, well, I don't like it," Zack muttered.

"Zack, mind your own business. You were literally sleeping with one of my closest friends behind my back. You have no room to talk or play big brother."

He frowned. "Play big brother? I am your big brother."

"You know what I mean."

The two of us had never been that close, but our relationship had improved since he started dating Bree. But if he thought he was going to be all protective over me, he could forget about it.

"Fine," Zack said with a sigh and dropped back down on the bed. I couldn't see him anymore, except for the arm that snaked around Bree's waist.

"Since it's no longer just the two of us, we'll talk later," Bree said.

"Tomorrow?" I offered.

"Tomorrow," she said. Then, she grinned and winked at me. "Have a fun night," she said in a singsong voice.

"I'd tell you the same, but I'd be too grossed out at even the notion," I replied in the same tone.

Bree laughed and said, "Night."

I grinned back. "Night."

I hung up my phone and threw it in front of me as Seth slid off my back.

"So, that was your brother?"

"Yeah."

"And your friend?"

"Yeah."

He seemed to be concentrating, and I realized what was probably bothering him.

I put my hand on his arm. "Don't worry. They won't tell anyone about us."

"Us?"

Shit. I'd made it sound like we were in a relationship.

"I mean, they won't say anything about you and me looking cozy and intimate." I didn't want him to worry anymore, so I crawled closer and kissed him. "They can keep a secret." I scoffed. *Boy, can they keep a secret.* "Trust me."

He surprised me by lifting a shoulder and saying, "I'm not even a little worried."

Chapter Twenty-One
SETH

TESSA WALKED TO THE BATHROOM, saying she was going to wash her face and brush her teeth, and I pushed myself off her bed and went into the main area.

Dinner wasn't sitting right with me, and I wanted to check on something on my computer.

It wasn't that I thought I wouldn't be prepared for the presentation meeting. It was that I didn't like Gene Ainsworth. I couldn't put my finger on why, but I felt my instincts were part of the reason I'd achieved as much as I had in my career. I wasn't going to ignore them now.

I pulled up a search engine and typed in *Gene Ainsworth and Spark Advertising* to see if anything came up. When I'd heard he'd dropped his old advertising agency, I could admit, all I had seen was the money Paragon would bring in. I hadn't looked into what had happened.

There were a few tech articles listed first, but they

didn't give any details, just the basics. But I didn't expect things like this to be front page news. Gene Ainsworth was rich. He had way more money than me, and he owned one of the biggest tech companies in the world. The man had a lot of power to keep information on the down-low.

It took some digging, but I finally saw something that caught my eye as a reason I might be concerned about working with the man, but it wasn't a news article. It was a tweet on Twitter.

It was on the day that the news had broken about Paragon leaving Spark behind.

Take note. The news is reporting that #paragon fired #sparkadvertising, but it is Spark that told Paragon—and more importantly, #geneainsworth—that they no longer wanted to work with him.

I did more digging but found nothing more than the single Twitter post, but that didn't stop me from having a sick feeling in my gut. I clenched and unclenched my hands. I had no proof that Gene Ainsworth had done anything out of line, but it didn't matter. If that man ever did one thing remotely questionable to Tessa, I would kill him.

I was thankful that I had never left her alone with him.

I slumped down in my seat and rubbed my forehead. I needed to decide if I was going to bring her to the Paragon building on Thursday. I needed to figure out if I even wanted to go to the meeting at all.

By securing this new account, I could afford to give all

my employees a raise, and with a vague post like that, I didn't know what had happened. I was only speculating.

I opened my email and found the CEO of Spark Advertising. Maybe if I contacted him—one CEO to another—I would get some information on Gene Ainsworth and Paragon.

There was a chance that someone might email me back tonight, but I doubted it, so I tried to put it out of my mind.

I opened a new tab in my browser and searched *Functional Bean Coffee Company*. And since this was a company and an owner I had heard nothing but good things about, I threw myself into preparing for tomorrow morning's phone meeting.

I ended up losing track of time until I suddenly looked at the corner of my computer and realized how late it was.

I was feeling good about the call in the morning and figured I could pack it in for the night. I could get up early if I thought of more information to add.

I shut off my laptop and closed the lid before heading to Tessa's room. I was hoping she was up, reading, so I could convince her to come to my room and get naked, but she was already sleeping. I wished I had thought to tell her to come to my bed earlier, as I had a king and she had a queen, but I had already slept in there once the first night we were here.

I stripped off my clothes and got down to my boxers

before climbing into bed next to her. I wasn't going to cuddle with her, afraid I'd wake her up. I simply wanted to be close to her, but she made small whimpers in her sleep.

My heart broke for her because she was having a bad dream. Again.

Since it didn't seem to be as bad as it had been the other night, I wrapped my arm around her and pulled her close but did not attempt to wake her.

Her body relaxed at first, and I was feeling hopeful my presence was calming, but then she cried out and stiffened.

"Tessa," I said, squeezing her close. "Tessa, it's okay. I'm here."

Her body jolted once, and then it was like she let every muscle go. She turned in my arms and tentatively touched my face. "Seth?"

"Yeah. I'm here now. I've got you."

She cupped my face and attacked my mouth with her kisses. Her tongue was like fire and full of impatience, as if she couldn't get enough of me.

I wasn't sure if it was the right thing to do after a bad dream, but I'd also had my share of nightmares, and wanting to feel good and in control of something after waking up from one seemed normal to me.

I held her close as she threw a leg over my hips and rubbed her pussy against my dick. She whimpered for a whole other reason this time.

She trailed one of her hands from my face down to my boxers. She wasted no time, slipping her hand underneath the band and grabbing my shaft.

I groaned into her mouth, and she bit my lip.

"Fuck," I muttered.

She removed her leg from my hip and pushed down at my boxers. I helped her by kicking them off while she went to work on her own pajama bottoms.

I was ready for a few more minutes of foreplay before we moved to the main event, but Tessa had other plans. She whipped her leg back over mine, grabbed my dick, and sank her sweet, incredibly hot, and wet pussy on it.

I had given myself a minute last night of feeling her bare pussy while she orgasmed, but I had immediately pulled out and put a condom on before we did anything else. So, I was a little bit of a hypocrite when it dawned on me that I should really stop us from going any further.

Except she felt so good, and I told myself, *Just a few more seconds, just a few more seconds*, several times.

God. She felt amazing, and knowing she wanted me this badly made it hard to say no.

And when she came apart in my arms, it made it all worth it.

I shoved my face in her neck and held back my orgasm while her pussy contracted around my cock. Not coming inside her was the hardest thing I had ever done in my life, and I was not invincible.

I brushed my lips against hers. "Tessa, baby, I can't hold on."

Her leg around my ass didn't loosen.

"Tessa, I'm not wearing a condom."

This seemed to get through to her, and she quickly rolled away.

I winced as my tender penis was pulled from her body, but I didn't climax. Ready to get myself off because I needed to finish or be in pain, I went to grab myself.

But Tessa practically flew down the bed, knocked away my hand, and sucked me into her mouth.

That was all it took for me to come, and while I couldn't do it in her pussy, on her tongue was a very pleasurable second.

I collapsed onto my back and closed my eyes once I was done. One round with Tessa, and I was exhausted.

She climbed back up my body and kissed me. I willingly opened my mouth for her, wanting to know what the two of us tasted like together.

"Mmm," I said as she pulled away.

"I'm sorry about the no-condom thing. I got a little caught up in the moment."

"It's okay. We survived."

She laughed lightly and laid her head on my shoulder.

I rubbed her back and kissed her forehead. "I've seen you sleeping four times, and three of those, you were having bad dreams. Do you get them every night?"

She tensed for a moment and said, "No."

That made me feel a little better, yet I hated that she had them at all. "Do you want to talk about it?"

Chapter Twenty-Two

TESSA

"NOT REALLY," I admitted. "But I might feel better if I talk about it."

It helped that it was dark and that I could still feel Seth between my legs and taste him on my tongue.

"No pressure," he said as he ran his hand up and down my back as we laid on our sides. "But maybe saying it out loud will help you process whatever is giving you nightmares."

"I'll give it a try. But just so you know, I don't have bad dreams every night or even almost every night." I kissed his chest. "In case you thought I did."

"I didn't think that. And even if you did, it's not a deal-breaker. No one is perfect."

You are, I thought.

"My dad worked in maintenance at a private high school. One of his job benefits was getting free tuition for his kids, so of course, my parents wanted private schooling for their children. My brother is older than me and had already gone there for a couple years, and he loved it, so I figured I would too."

"But you didn't," Seth already guessed.

"But I didn't," I agreed. "My parents were—are—working class. I grew up in a small, modest home, where my parents were blue-collar workers. I still remember how some months, they had to really scrimp to pay the bills, but we had a roof over our heads, so I didn't mind. And all my friends in the neighborhood were like me. But going to a private school was different."

"I bet."

"There were some middle-class kids, and then there were the rich upper-class kids. The only thing was that the middle-class kids might not have had fancy cars or houses with pools in the backyard, but they could still wear the right clothes and buy the cool stuff that everyone else had."

"And you couldn't."

I snorted. "Not even close. But neither could my brother. So, at first, I didn't think it was a big deal, except it soon made sense why his friends never came over to our house. Anyway, the difference was, my brother played football, wrestled, and was good-looking. He dated a cheerleader or two and got invited to all the cool parties. But I was not athletic, and with the size of these hips, I was considered overweight."

Technically, if you asked my doctor, I was still overweight, but the difference between then and now was, I had grown into my figure and wore my curves with confidence. Confidence a fourteen-year-old kid did not have.

I took a deep breath before the next part because it was embarrassing. "They called me Bessa."

"Bessa?"

"It's a clever nickname. It's a combination of Bessy and Tessa. You know...Bessy, as in cow."

"Oh damn."

"Yeah. So, I was overweight, poor, and uncool."

"Didn't your brother do anything to defend you?"

"He didn't know. Not the full extent of it anyway. They kept the grades relatively separated, so he wasn't around to witness anything. He knew I didn't like it there, but he didn't really understand why."

"I still feel like he should have done something."

Even telling my story, I had to smile. "You're sweet, but he really didn't know. All the kids who made fun of me were freshman, like me. The older kids didn't even know who I was. We even did lunch with only our own grade."

"I can see how he wouldn't know."

"Anyway, as you can probably guess, no one wanted to be friends with me because they didn't want to get made fun of too. I was lonely and alone. But the last straw was gym, when we started swimming. After everyone saw me in a suit, the teasing got worse. One day after class, which was the last one of the day, a bunch of kids cornered me after the teacher left right away because of an emergency. They pushed me into this thing that was part cupboard, part closet and locked me in. And the teacher didn't come back for over two hours. I was lucky she'd left her things behind and found me, or I would have been stuck there all night."

Seth rolled on his back and pulled me close. "Oh my God, Tessa. That's awful."

"It is. The only good thing was, I went home and begged—*begged*—my mother to let me go back to public school. She never asked me why, but she's smart; I think she knew something bad had happened. She said yes, and I never went back."

"Shit. I'm glad about that."

"Yeah. I met some good kids at my public high school. And sure, there were still kids with money, but it wasn't the majority, and they didn't give me a hard time every day."

"Kids are fucking assholes."

I chuckled. "Yes, they are."

"So, you mentioned the rich kids a lot. And I noticed you didn't like Alexis's ex…"

Seth was observant.

"Alexis's ex would be a dick even if he didn't have money, but yes, I've always had a bias against rich people. I almost didn't come to work for you."

Seth pulled back to look at me better even though it was dark in my room. "No shit?"

"It's true."

"What made you change your mind?"

"Alexis and our business. The pay was too good to pass up." I snorted. "How hypocritical of me."

"I grew up in a middle-class home, but I remember there were times when something big would happen, like the air conditioner would go out or we needed a new fridge, and my parents would worry about how they were going to pay for it. So, I can say, it's one thing to seek out money when you need it, but it's another thing to seek it out when you already have a lot. That's one of the reasons I try to pay my employees well. I don't want them to have to live paycheck to paycheck."

I had wondered about that since Seth was paying me a good rate. I had also noticed that he didn't force people to work long hours, except when the Paragon account had come up.

"Will you stay here and sleep with me tonight?" I asked.

"Nah."

Oh. I hadn't expected that answer. *Ouch.* After everything I told him.

I took a deep, calming breath. *It's okay, Tessa. He's not your boyfriend. He doesn't have to stay.*

I rolled away from him and attempted to play it cool. "Well, I promise to have no more bad dreams tonight."

He pushed the covers off him and stood.

Damn, he's sexy.

Despite my disappointment, I couldn't stop admiring him. He turned and stuck his head under the sheet and dug near the bottom of the bed, and it made me smile. I wondered if that meant I was in trouble where Seth Crawford was concerned.

"What are you doing?"

He stood and held up our clothes with a grin. "Looking for our clothes."

My face heated as I remembered how I'd attacked him. "Right." I held out my hands for my pajama bottoms. "Thank you for finding them."

He set them on the bed rather than giving them to me. "You don't need these. You look better without them."

That warmed my heart and helped ease the disappointment. "Thanks."

"Now, if you lose the top, you'll be complete."

What was the point since I'd be sleeping alone?

"Again, thank you, but I'm not planning on doing any fashion shows."

"Just a private one for me." He smirked. "In bed."

I stared at him, confused.

He jerked his head toward the door. "Come on. Let's go."

I still didn't get it.

He sighed and came over to my side of the bed. He whipped the comforter off of me and picked me up in a fireman hold.

I screeched. "Seth, what are you doing?"

"Taking you to my bed since your legs don't seem to work. But then again, they shouldn't work after a good fuck."

"They work just fine."

Seth gasped mockingly. "How dare you."

I laughed. "But why are we going to your room?"

He dropped me down onto his bed, where I bounced. "Two reasons. King-size bed and condoms. I figured it was easier for us to spend the night in here."

I grinned. "So, you're saying, you want me to sleep with you?" I asked coyly.

"Duh." He raised his brow. "Although I can't promise you'll be getting that much sleep."

Chapter Twenty-Three
TESSA

THE NEXT MORNING, Seth got up early while I slept in. Since the meeting wasn't until nine, I was taking my time, getting up and getting ready. I could take notes in my PJs just as easily as I could in business clothes.

Because of this, I took a shower, put on the fluffy bathrobe provided by the hotel, and lay on my bed to read. Thankfully, Seth hadn't done any damage to my paperback, so he was still in my good graces.

Around eight-thirty, he came into my room. "You look comfortable."

I was on my stomach, so I rolled up onto my side to see him better. "I am." I looked at the clock. "We have some time before your phone meeting, so I thought I would relax. Do you need me to do something? I was planning to listen in and take notes," I told him so he wouldn't think I was totally lazy.

He grabbed my calf and flipped me on my back.

Pushing my legs open, he rested his upper body on the mattress and said, "I wouldn't say I need anything, but since we have some time, I thought we might have a little fun."

"What do you have in—"

Seth shoved his head between my legs and licked.

"Mmm." I dropped my book and slipped a hand in my robe, so I could pinch my nipple.

Seth's phone rang on the dresser, where he had set it.

"No," I whined.

"Ignore it," Seth said.

I was about to, but something clicked in my brain. "Seth, what if it's Ryan Jackman's office? Maybe they're calling early for something?"

He groaned and stood, adjusting himself in his pants.

I closed the bottom half of my robe while he picked up his phone.

"Crap. You might be right."

I held out my hand, so I could answer for him, but he hit a button and said, "Seth Crawford speaking."

He smiled. "Mr. Jackman, it's a pleasure."

I moved to scramble off the bed, but Seth stepped forward and held up his hand.

I didn't understand.

And I still didn't get it when he put up a finger in the universal symbol for *I'll be right back.*

I flopped back on the bed and waited for him to come back.

He returned in just a few seconds with...a row of condoms.

My eyes widened in wonder of what he was going to do next.

He ripped one off with his teeth, threw them on the bed, and stripped off his shirt. Then, he undid his pants, opened the wrapper, and put the rubber on his dick. During this time, he didn't stop talking to Ryan Jackman, but I had lost track of what they were talking about.

A girl could not be expected to pay attention to a phone conversation and her lover's naked body at the same time.

Seth grasped my ankle and pulled me to the end of the bed while I had to bite back a squeak of surprise.

When my ass reached the end, he flipped open my robe again and slid his cock into me.

I immediately tightened around him and arched my neck as I bit my lip.

He felt unbelievably good, but I did have enough sense to remember he was on the phone, so I didn't make any noise.

I didn't know what kind of game Seth was playing right now, but at the moment, I was all in for whatever he wanted to do.

As he talked, he gently slid in and out of me. He was slow and methodical, and I understood why, but it was making me squirm.

He licked a thumb and placed it between my legs,

landing right on my clit. I had to give this man props for never having to search for it.

I tried to keep my eyes open, so I could watch him, but they soon fluttered closed, and I completely forgot he was in the middle of an important meeting.

He stopped moving and whispered my name, and I blinked my eyes open.

He grinned, shoved his phone between his shoulder and chin, and put a finger to his lips.

Oops. I hadn't even realized I was making noise.

As he continued to leisurely stroke his shaft inside me and circle my bundle of nerves, I kept my eyes open to watch him, hoping it would help me stay quiet.

But it didn't help.

Even though there was no rush to Seth's lovemaking, I was still getting closer and closer to coming. I tried to fight it, but it wasn't working. I also couldn't seem to stay quiet.

Seth's brow furrowed at something Ryan Jackman had said, and he said, "Oh, sure. Yes. Yes," as he slid a hand up and around my neck. It wasn't enough to cut off air, but it was enough to cut off my voice.

And now that his upper body was closer to mine, his strokes got deeper until I couldn't take it anymore.

My arms flung up, and I grabbed on to his arms and dug my nails in. My orgasm washed over me in a white-hot heat so hard that I could feel myself contract around him.

There was a soft grunt from Seth, and he tightened his hand a little more around my neck. I couldn't quite keep myself quiet.

When my orgasm gradually passed, my arms fell to my sides, and I caught the end of the conversation.

"That sounds great. I look forward to it." Pause. "Next month it is."

Seth hit a button, threw his phone on the bed, and dropped his body over mine. He lifted my hip with a hand and grabbed my hair with the other as he let go of everything he'd been holding back.

He pounded into me so hard that I swore he rearranged my cervix. But it was all good. After the gentleness, I was ready for a rough ride. I was also ready to make all the sounds I wanted, and I moaned into his ear to encourage him.

It wasn't long before he slammed into me twice and exploded. I held him as he rode his wave of pleasure.

When he lifted his head, he brushed my hair from my face and said, "You okay?"

Was I okay? That was the hottest fuck I had ever had.

"That depends," I teased.

His eyebrows flew up. "On what?"

"On whether or not you got the account."

He grinned and kissed me. "Oh, I fucking got the account all right."

I'd pretty much already known he did, but I needed to hear it. "Does this mean you have a big head now?"

"How so?"

"You just gave me the best orgasm of my life while scoring a new account with a famous actor."

"That depends," he said, returning my words to me.

"On what?"

"On whether or not you still want to have Ryan Jackman's babies."

"Who the hell is Ryan Jackman?"

Chapter Twenty-Four

TESSA

THE NEXT AFTERNOON, we were supposed to be leaving for the meeting with Paragon, but Seth kept refreshing his email.

"What is going on?" I asked him. "We need to go soon, or we'll be late."

He sighed. "I emailed the CEO of Spark Advertising over twenty-four hours ago about Paragon, but I haven't heard anything back yet."

"I'm sorry to tell you this, but I don't think he's going to email you in the next two minutes. Also, won't you get the email on your phone?"

"I know. And, yes, you're right."

"What was your email concerning?"

Seth ran his hand over his fauxhawk. "I didn't get the best impression of Gene Ainsworth, and I wanted to know what had happened between him and Spark." He met my eyes. "I know you didn't get the best impression of him either."

"You're right; I didn't. But it was one meeting. Maybe he was having an off night." I stepped toward Seth and put my hands on his chest. "Just because you go to this meeting today doesn't mean you have to work with him. You know how I always look at things?"

He gave me a half-smile. "How?"

"Ask yourself if you'll regret going today. My guess is, probably not. So we waste a few hours in this meeting." I shrugged. "So what?" I poked him. "But then ask yourself if you will regret not going. I would say, you have a higher chance of regretting that. This is a big account for you and your company. Don't you at least want to hear what he has to say?"

"No," Seth grumbled.

I raised my brow.

"Okay, maybe a little."

"Let's go then. Before it's too late."

"You're right." He pulled the presentation items off the table. "Let's go."

———

We got to the Paragon building only five minutes early, which didn't look the best if you asked me, but at least we made it before the agreed-upon meeting time.

Someone from the company came to the lobby and took us upstairs. The gentleman didn't say much, just showed us to the conference room and then excused himself.

We were the only ones there, and Seth and I took the opportunity to set up our presentation.

"If he comes in here and tells us we're moving to a different room," I said, "I'm going to be mad."

Seth chuckled. "Even with my reservations, I doubt he would do something like that."

We were almost finished when Gwyneth Ainsworth walked in. "Hello, Mr. Crawford, Ms. Archer."

"Hello, Ms. Ainsworth," Seth said.

"Good afternoon," I said.

Gwyneth turned back to Seth. "Mr. Crawford, I was instructed to show you to the tech room."

I looked at Seth. I thought he had just said they were unlikely to make us change rooms.

"Oh no," Gwyneth said, holding out her hands. "You're still having the meeting here. I will just be taking you for a quick tour."

I breathed a sigh of relief.

"Are you ready?" Gwyneth asked Seth. "Or do you need to finish up first?"

"No, we're good to go."

"I'm sorry, but only you can come."

Seth looked at me.

"It's for liability reasons," Gwyneth said.

I waved him off. "It's fine. Go. Look around. I'll be right here when you're done."

Seth mulled it over and finally said, "Fine. Lead the way."

The two left, and I rechecked everything to make sure we hadn't forgotten anything.

I heard the door click behind me.

"You're done alre—" I turned to see Gene Ainsworth standing in front of the closed conference door.

I smiled, but it wasn't with as much confidence as I would have liked.

"Hello, Ms. Archer."

"Hello," I said, moving so the large conference table was between us.

"I was glad to hear that you were here this afternoon, but I was disappointed that you hadn't contacted me about sightseeing."

I had to hold in my shudder of revulsion.

"Se—Mr. Crawford and I were busy yesterday. We had another meeting to attend." Sure, it had been completed by noon, but I was not about to tell this man that Seth and I had gone swimming in the hotel pool and then upstairs to make love.

Mr. Ainsworth tsked. "That's too bad." He stepped forward to come around to my side of the table, but I didn't retreat, as he was still at the other end. "I was looking forward to showing you around." His smile was dripping with sexuality.

I wanted to vomit.

"Sorry, Mr. Crawford likes to keep me close," I said curtly, trying to throw hints to leave me alone.

Mr. Ainsworth advanced on me, and I looked to the door.

Please, Seth, come back soon.

Seth

"We need to go back," I said, cutting off Gwyneth Ainsworth as she showed me some piece of a phone that I cared not one single thing about.

"But we're not finished," she said.

"I don't care. Take me back to the conference room."

She hesitated.

"*Now.*"

She nodded and led me out the door and back the way we had come.

As we walked, she wrung her hands. "Did I do something wrong?"

I frowned. "No."

"Then, why—"

"Because something's not right, and I don't feel comfortable, leaving Ms. Archer alone."

Gwyneth's head dropped, and I got the impression she knew something.

When we got close, the first thing I noticed was the door to the conference room was closed.

I marched forward and practically threw it open.

The first thing I saw was Gene Ainsworth's arms around Tessa and his mouth on hers.

Then, I saw red.

I must have made an angry sound because Gene jumped back and held his hands up in surrender.

"I am sorry, but your assistant came on to me. I know I should have said no, but she is very beautiful."

Tessa gasped, and her eyes flew to mine, pleading with me to believe her.

"Let's go, Tessa," I said.

She looked at the presentation items.

"Leave them."

"But, Seth, all this hard work."

"I don't fucking care." I pointed to the floor. "Get over here now."

Tessa put her head down and came to my side. "I'm sorry," she whispered.

My brow furrowed. *What the fuck?*

"If you would like to see your assistant back to the hotel and come back here, we can finish our meeting," Gene said.

I looked at him in shock. This guy had some big brass balls. Unfortunately, he used them for the wrong thing.

"If you think I'm coming back here, you need a reality check." I grabbed Tessa's hand and strode toward the door.

We passed Gwyneth, who stood there with her mouth agape.

Tessa and I kept going, but Gwyneth ran after us.

"Please, don't go. He's—he's not right."

I let go of Tessa's hand and spun around. Pointing my finger in Gwyneth's direction, I said, "You're correct; he's not right. But neither are you if you continue to leave him in charge."

"He's...he's my father."

"And a liability." I did feel for her because she seemed genuinely distraught. "In this building, you need to figure out if you're his daughter or the future of this company. You can't be both. But honestly, I wouldn't even want that man running around as my father." I pivoted on my heel. "Let's go, Tessa. We're done here."

Chapter Twenty-Five

TESSA

SETH DIDN'T SAY a single word on our way back to the hotel. It was the most awkward silence I had ever experienced in my life.

The Uber driver tried to make conversation a couple of times, but when I gave polite, one-worded answers and Seth only grunted, he gave up.

When we got to the hotel, Seth exited the vehicle first and held the door open for me, but he wouldn't look me in the eye.

I was already worried because I wasn't sure what he thought he'd seen back there. When Gene Ainsworth had put his hands on me, I had been ready to slap him for touching me, job or no job, but Seth had burst through the door first.

I felt sick to my stomach.

The elevator ride up was just as bad as the car ride. The silence was deafening.

I didn't know what to do or say. I wished Seth would just talk to me.

He unlocked the suite door, and once again, he held it open for me, but his gaze was directed at the big windows facing the street. He let go, and the door shut with a loud click behind us.

"Seth..."

He walked past me and went into his room, where he slammed the door.

My shoulders sagged. He wasn't even going to let me explain.

Feeling defeated, I went to my own bedroom, not knowing what else to do. I sat down on the bed and stared at the wall, unsure of where to go from here.

There was a ring that made me jump, and it took me a minute to realize it was the hotel phone.

"Hello?" I answered.

"This is Doug. I believe we spoke the day of your arrival."

It took me a second. "Oh, yes. Yes, Doug. How can I help you?"

"Well, ma'am, I believe I can help you." I could hear the smile in his voice. "We just had a room open up. It's a single—"

I started laughing.

"Ma'am, are you okay?"

I pursed my lips to try to stop, but the timing couldn't have been any better. I also knew I was laughing because it beat crying.

"I'm sorry. I'm okay." I huffed out a big breath. "You were saying?"

"We have a single room. It has a king-size bed and—"

"I'll take it."

"You don't need to hear anything else?"

"Nope. I'll take it."

"Excellent. Shall I expect you soon?"

I looked around. I needed to pack up my stuff in the bedroom and the bathroom. I also needed my computer and a couple of other things in the main room. "Give me a half hour. Will that work?"

"Yes. I will see you in a half hour."

I hung up and closed my eyes. While the hotel room was a relief, I still felt sick about what had happened at Paragon.

I was pretty sure I was out of a job, so there went the down payment Alexis and I needed. I had flown to California on the company's money, but now, I was going to have to fly to Minneapolis on my own dime. But the worst part was, Seth probably hated me.

I had completely ruined everything.

I straightened my spine. *One thing at a time.*

First things first. I needed to get packed and out of there. At least I wouldn't have to face Seth's disappointment anymore. Once I was settled in my own room—which I was also going to have to pay for myself—I could figure out the rest.

I couldn't afford to stay in California more than one

night. We were going home anyway, but now, I needed to book the first flight back to Minnesota.

I found my phone and turned on some music, hoping it would calm me some. Then, I set my suitcase on the bed and began folding my clothes.

When I finished with my clothes, I turned to head to the bathroom to pack those items next but gasped when I saw Seth, standing in my doorway.

My music wasn't loud, but I hadn't heard him coming toward my room, and I wasn't prepared to see him. I had wanted to leave before he came out of his bedroom.

"What are you doing?" he asked in a low voice.

I scrambled for my phone and quickly turned it off.

I pushed my hair behind my ear. "I'm packing up. The front desk found me another room. I'll be out of your hair in about fifteen minutes."

Seth did that thing where he simply watched me and didn't speak. He stood perfectly still, and I had no idea what he was thinking.

Shifting from one foot to the other, I said, "I'll also get my own flight back home, and I can go into the office Monday morning and turn in my badge and pick up my personal items."

He turned away and rubbed his chin. He looked so strong and handsome, and I wanted to throw myself into his arms and cry.

Why couldn't he have stayed in his bedroom for just a little bit longer?

It didn't matter now, and the only thing I could do was finish collecting my things and get out of there.

I headed for the bathroom. "Excuse me," I said, trying to slip past him.

He stopped me by shooting his arm out and resting it on the doorframe.

I didn't attempt to keep moving, but I couldn't look at him.

"I'm sorry," he said in a low voice.

My head jerked up. "What?"

"I'm sorry. I knew something wasn't right, but I let you come with me today anyway. I should have never done that."

I fell back against the open door. "You're not mad at me?"

Fire burned in his eyes. "Why the fuck would I be mad at you? I'm mad at myself. And I'm very angry with Paragon and the Ainsworths. But, no, I'm not angry with you."

"But you..." I looked down at my feet. "But you wouldn't touch me. Or speak to me. And when we got back here, you slammed the door when you went to your room." I took a deep breath and lifted my chin. "I know I messed this deal up for you. I'm the one who's sorry."

Seth moved so fast that I yelped. He caged me against the door with his hands over my head and his body pressed against mine.

"I need you to listen to me," he said.

I nodded.

"You did nothing wrong. I know that he touched you without consent. I know you wouldn't willingly involve yourself with that asshole." He dropped his forehead to mine. "You have nothing to be sorry for."

"But—"

"No *buts*. I didn't touch you or say anything because we were in public and all I wanted to do was take you to bed. I had to go in my own room and calm down. Because I want to kiss away his touch and replace it with my own. I want to come all over you and in you to let him know he needs to stay away." He rubbed his nose against mine. "It's not rational. It's not romantic. And it's selfish of me and not very considerate of you."

I wrapped my arms around his neck. "I want the same thing."

Seth growled, picked me up in his arms, and carried me to his bed.

Chapter Twenty-Six

SETH

TESSA and I exited the airplane and headed toward baggage claim.

"You remembered to tell your brother not to pick you up?" I asked.

"Yes. I told him that I was getting a ride from you."

Seeing as her brother seemed a little protective of her, I also asked, "And how did he take it?"

"He didn't care. It saved him the trip of coming here."

Maybe I was wrong. "Some brother," I said.

She laughed. "Okay, real truth. I didn't tell him. I told his girlfriend, and she told him. And then he sent me a text, telling me to be careful."

"Why didn't you say so?"

She shrugged. "I don't want my brother and...my boss to not like one another."

I wanted to throw my arm around her and kiss her, but

we were in public and back in Minnesota. I didn't need word to get out that I was sleeping with my assistant.

"Actually, I like your brother more now, knowing he worries about you." I stepped a little closer. "And I'm more than your boss."

She looked up at me. "Yeah, I know; you're my friend."

I snorted. "I'm also your lover," I corrected in a low voice.

Her eyes rounded. "Does that mean we're going to continue this now that we're home?"

"You bet your ass we are. I thought I'd made it pretty apparent last night that I want you for more than just the week."

She blushed and looked away in embarrassment.

After I'd caught Tessa packing and I'd cleared up the misunderstanding, I'd made love to her. Holding her in my arms all night had helped to push away the vision of Ainsworth putting his hands on her, but it would probably take some time for me to not feel like punching a wall every time I thought of it.

"But if you don't feel the same way, I want you to know, there will be no consequences at work or otherwise. The ball is completely in your court."

"Can I decide later?" she asked with a smile.

"Why? What are you thinking?"

"It's Friday, which means it's the weekend. Can we just pretend we're still on vacation and make real-life decisions on Monday?"

"If that means you're spending the night at my place, the answer is yes."

She cringed.

"What?"

"I need to get back to my place. My neighbor has been taking care of my cats, but she went out of town for the weekend." She bit her lip. "I know. I can go home, feed my cats, and come to your place."

I shrugged. "Or we can just spend the night at your house?" I liked the idea of being in her home.

"You saw my house the day you dropped me off, right?"

I laughed. "The outside, yes."

"It's small. I have three tiny bedrooms. I don't know if you're going to like it there."

"I'm going to love it," I said.

———

After Tessa and I picked up our luggage, we went outside to wait for the car service I'd ordered. I liked Uber when I was out of town, but when I was in the Twin Cities area, I liked to use one particular business that always did a good job. The driver already had my address and knew where to go. I needed to drop off my luggage and get some clean clothes.

When we pulled up to my apartment, Tessa asked, "Where are we?"

"My building."

"Do you have more than one home?"

I frowned and shook my head. "No." I got out of the car, and I helped the driver unload our stuff from the trunk.

After I tipped the driver, he took off, and Tessa looked around, as if she was wondering what to do.

"Sorry, but my vehicle is in the parking garage down below. We'll have to take your stuff upstairs for a few minutes."

"That is not my problem," she said.

I raised my brow. "Your problem? I wasn't aware you had one."

She stomped her foot. "Seth, the day you took me home after work, you told me you lived close."

I laughed, having completely forgotten about that. "Sorry. I knew you wouldn't let me take you home if you knew where I lived, and you were too tired to drive."

"I could have called a ride."

I grabbed the handle of my suitcase and headed for the front of the building. "You wouldn't have though," I pointed out.

Tessa followed me into the building.

"Wow," she said. "This place is state of the art."

I smiled and said, "Come on." After being on the airplane and losing two hours, I really wanted to get to her place.

In the elevator, I pressed the button for the top floor.

"Let me guess...you live in the penthouse."

"I do."

Her eyes bugged out. "I was joking. This isn't New York. I didn't think those existed in Minnesota."

I chuckled. "Well, they do."

We got to my apartment, and the look of wonder continued to show on her face. I knew I needed to get out of there as soon as possible before she started to worry again about the difference in how much money we had. I quickly packed some new clothes and exited my bedroom.

"Do you own the place?" she asked when I entered the room.

"Actually, I rent. I guess I always pictured living in a house one day. It's just that right now, when it's just me, it's easier to live here, in an apartment in the city."

She snorted. "*Apartment* is a loose term."

I flung my backpack with my clean clothes over my shoulder and took her hand. "Come on. Let's get out of here."

―――

When we got to her place, she opened the door and took a deep breath. She was happy to be home.

I never felt that way about my apartment.

"Come in," Tessa said. "The cats try to get outside if the door is open too long."

Her house was small, but it was homey. It reminded me of my home, growing up, and I already knew I was going to like spending time here.

"Go ahead and sit down. I'm going to take my suitcase

upstairs. If you see two furballs, they won't hurt you, but they might yell at you some."

Tessa went upstairs, and I took my cell out of my pocket as I lay back on her sofa. I kept waiting to hear something from Paragon, but so far, they'd been silent. And I never hadn't heard from Spark Advertising.

I was scanning my emails when something hard landed on my balls.

I grunted and moved my phone to see what had happened.

"*Meow.*"

"Holy crap, you are heavy."

The black-and-white cat began to knead my crotch.

"Oh, so now, you're trying to make up for hurting me, huh?" I scratched him or her behind one ear.

Tessa came back down a few minutes later. "Oh, I see you found Persephone."

"More like Persephone found me. She jumped on my junk."

Tessa laughed and came over to pet the cat. "Persephone, how dare you! I have plans for that junk later."

Persephone lay down on my lap, and I snorted. "I think I made a friend."

"Don't get too cocky. She likes everyone." She looked at her cat. "Persephone, where's Hades?"

"*Meow,*" Persephone said, and a second later, another meow sounded behind her. She turned, and there was a big, fluffy orange cat.

"Hades," Tessa said and scooped up the furball. "Are you hungry? Did you miss me?"

Hades turned his head away, looking unimpressed.

Tessa shrugged and put the cat down. "That's about all the love I get from Hades."

"He's the ruler of the underworld. What did you expect?"

"You're right. I need to adjust my expectations. Obviously, it's my fault," she said dryly.

I picked Persephone up and set her next to me, and then I pulled Tessa down to my lap. "Don't worry. I will give you plenty of love later."

Tessa cocked her eyebrows, and I chuckled.

Yeah, I had used the word *love*, and I wasn't going to take it back.

Chapter Twenty-Seven

TESSA

PAISLEY CLUTCHED her hands to her chest. "So, he just gave up the whole deal for you?"

I blushed. "I don't think he gave it all up for *me* per se. I mean, as Seth said to Ainsworth's daughter, the guy is a liability."

Paisley waved me away. "Let me have my romantic thoughts."

The rest of us—Alexis, Bree, Pru, Isabelle, Elizabeth, and me—laughed.

"You are a hopeless romantic, girl," Pru said.

"I know," Paisley admitted with a sigh.

Not only had Seth given up the deal, but he'd also spent all weekend at my house. He cooked dinner on Saturday and helped me clean up after we finished eating. I'd expected someone like him to not be used to doing housework, but he didn't act like it was a big deal at all.

He went home on Sunday night because we both

decided it would be better for us not to show up to work at the same time on Monday morning. It was the first night I'd slept alone in almost a week, and I hated how much I'd missed him.

Which was why I told him I wanted to keep seeing him. I didn't care if we had to keep it a secret at work. I wasn't going to be there forever, and it would be worth it if I got to see him every day.

Monday, Seth had been so busy, meeting with the team who had worked on the Paragon proposal and then making an announcement to the whole office, that I hardly saw him.

Tuesday and Wednesday were busy too. We snuck a few kisses here and there, but it wasn't the same as working out of the hotel room. It was a good thing we'd still spent the night together on Monday and Tuesday.

It was Wednesday night, and since it was my monthly dinner with my friends, I told him I'd see him tomorrow.

Bree poked me in the arm. "You remember how much crap you gave me for dating your brother and breaking the 'rule' of our club? I think I should give you the same amount of shit back now that you're in a relationship."

I held up my hands. "Whoa, whoa, whoa. Seth and I are not in a relationship. I don't think I'd even classify it as seeing each other. We're just having fun."

"Yeah, in the bedroom," Alexis said.

Everyone laughed, including me.

"Exactly," I said. "Seth asked me if I wanted to continue this thing we had going when we got back home.

He offered me a choice, which I appreciated instead of him just assuming it would be ongoing. But it's not like he's confessed his undying love for me or anything."

"I guess we'll see," Bree said.

"To tell you the truth, I don't know if it can last after I quit. We're having fun right now, and we're in the honeymoon phase, but once that wears off, it's going to be apparent that he makes so much more money than me. I can't do everything he does and go everywhere he goes. And I refuse to let him pay for me to go places with him. It will get old for both of us."

Paisley frowned, and her lower lip protruded. "That's so depressing."

"No, it's life. Pais, we started this club for a reason. I'm simply having a little fun right now, but I am still as single as ever." I agreed it was sad, but I wanted to go into this with my eyes wide open. I was already preparing myself for the end.

"Well, get him to take you on another trip for work before it's too late," Elizabeth said.

I laughed. "I'll get right on that."

Alexis's phone beeped next to her, and mine went off a second later.

"Is that Seth?" Isabelle asked me.

I picked up my cell. "No, it's from our realtor."

"Uh-oh, I got a text too," Alexis said.

> Jana: Sorry for the late text, but I just found out the strip mall is going up for sale early. There is a buyer interested in several of the stores, including the one that you both have your eye on. Let's talk tomorrow and discuss our next steps.

My good mood shattered, and Alexis looked like she wanted to cry.

"What happened?" Pru asked.

I gently set my phone facedown, so I wouldn't have to look at the awful message. "The building we want is going up for sale early because they have an interested buyer."

"And we are nowhere near having enough money for the down payment," Alexis said in an almost-monotone voice, as if she was in shock.

"I don't understand," Bree said. "It wasn't supposed to be up for sale for another month or so."

"Money," I said. "Some rich person wants it, so that rich person is going to get it." I clenched my fists in frustration.

We were still somewhere between five to ten thousand dollars short, and there was no way we were going to be able to scrape that much together within a couple of days.

I swallowed my sadness and tried to look at the bright side. "It sucks. It really does, but Alexis and I will find a new place. It might not be as good as this one, but we will find a space for our dream."

"There are several stores in the strip mall. Can't you pick another one?" Bree asked.

Alexis shook her head. "They're all spoken for, so the chance of one of them being on the market by the time we have our money together is very slim."

The table was full of sad ladies now, and no one seemed to know what to say to make things better.

"I know we're going to lose our first pick for location, but I got an idea for something for our place when I was in San Francisco."

Alexis looked hopeful even though she had to know that I wasn't going to magically come up with money. "What's that?"

"What if our place was not just a bakery and a café, but also a cat café?"

I held my breath as I waited for Alexis to say no.

"Oh my God, I love that idea."

I squealed as I opened my arms, and she hugged me.

"I was so afraid you'd shoot it down."

She pulled back. "Why would you think that?"

"I don't know. Because you don't have any cats."

"That's because my ex never wanted them, and now, I live in an apartment that doesn't allow pets. I think it's an awesome idea."

"We're going to have to think of a whole new name," I warned.

Alexis chuckled. "We haven't even come up with one in the first place."

"This is true," I said with a grin.

Bree lifted her glass. "Even though we had some bad news tonight, I think we should still cheers to the cat café."

"I agree," Elizabeth said.

"I was already planning to be there constantly," Paisley said. "But now, I might just move in."

"Thanks, ladies, for making us feel better," I said.

"That's what friends are for," Bree said.

Now, if we could come up with a miracle for a new location soon, life would be pretty darn good.

Chapter Twenty-Eight

SETH

THURSDAY MORNING, I got to work before most of my employees, including Tessa, and I was concentrating, so I didn't hear her arrival until my office door opened and closed.

She came into the room, set my latte down, and turned around to go back without even meeting my eyes. She seemed to be in a daze.

"Hey," I said.

She stopped and turned.

"No good-morning kiss?"

She smiled. "Sorry. I just have something on my mind."

I pushed my chair back from my desk. "Come here."

She came over, and I took her hand and pulled her in for a kiss. "I missed you last night."

"I missed you too."

"Liar. You barely gave me a single glance this morning," I teased her.

"Hey, I got you coffee. So, you clearly must have been on my mind."

"What's going on?" I asked.

She leaned back against my desk. "Last night, Alexis and I found out we might lose our location."

I winced. "Oh, that's rough. What happened?"

She explained the text she and Alexis had received last night. "We still don't have enough funds, so we're supposed to meet with our realtor after one p.m. to figure out our next steps. Do you mind if I leave to do that? I'll be back later in the afternoon to finish work."

"Not at all." I tilted my head. "Do you mind if I ask how short you are?"

"No, it's fine. Alexis and I did the math last night, and if we pool all our money, we're short six thousand dollars. But then we won't have anything left over if something comes up, like fees or other things." She put her fingers to her temples and rubbed.

I hated to say it, but six thousand was easy money for me. When she had said they were short on funds, I'd pictured a much larger number in my head. "I can give you six thousand."

Her head whipped up, her eyes wide.

"I can give you more than that, too, so you're not left without anything extra, if you want."

She stood. "Absolutely not."

I held up my hands. "Okay, I understand. How about

we consider it a loan? You can pay me back whenever you have the money, interest-free."

"No." She went to the other side of my desk. "I know you are offering out of the goodness of your heart, but the answer is no."

I rose from my chair. "Why?"

"Because..."

"Because why?"

"Because it just wouldn't be right, and it wouldn't work out, and it would just make a mess of everything."

"That is not a good explanation," I pointed out.

"Please, just drop it."

I hated for her to lose the place she wanted so badly, but I also didn't want to upset her any further. "Consider it dropped."

"Thank you. Now, if you don't mind, I'm going to get some work done before I have to meet with the realtor."

———

Tessa didn't say much the rest of the morning and only stopped in for a second to tell me she was leaving. I couldn't tell if she was preoccupied with her business problem or if she was upset with me for offering to give her the money. It was hard to tell because she'd been worried before she even spoke to me. But only time would tell.

She arrived back at the office a couple hours later and came straight to my door. Her purse fell off her shoulder, and she dragged it behind her as she walked to my couch and sat.

The meeting must not have gone well.

I left my desk, shut the door, and sat down next to her. "That bad, huh?"

She fell into my chest and nodded. "I keep telling myself we'll find another place, but I can't help but feel sad."

I wrapped my arm around her. "You have every right to feel disappointed. It's hard to find a good spot sometimes. But I'm sure another will come along," I quickly added.

"Did anything like this happen to you?"

I smiled. "No, but we worked out of John's house in the beginning. We'd rent conference rooms at hotels for cheap when we had to meet with clients."

"Oh yeah," she said. "The conference-room thing was smart."

"We sure thought it was. Some of our clients questioned it though."

Tessa lifted her head. "Whatever happened to John?"

My smile fell, and I looked away. "He died."

"Oh my God, I'm sorry."

"Me too." So much that I didn't want to talk about it. I looked at Tessa again. "Since you won't let me give you money, how about I keep an ear out for new and upcoming locations that might work for you?"

She slumped back in against the couch. "For about five seconds after meeting with our realtor, I honestly thought about taking you up on your offer, so don't think your generosity went unnoticed."

"If you change your mind, the offer still stands."

She put her hand in mine and squeezed. "Thank you, but I'll pass. I will take you up on the second offer though, where you keep your ears peeled."

"Done."

"Well, I'd better get back to work, so my boss doesn't get mad at me for slacking on the job."

I laughed and helped her up.

As she walked toward the door, an idea came to me.

"You know, at the end of every quarter, the company gives out bonuses."

She turned and looked at me like she wasn't fooled. "Nice try. But if you pay me more than my agreed-upon amount, I will just give it back to you."

I laughed. "Can't blame a guy for wanting to help his girl."

"Your girl, huh?"

"Yeah, my girl."

"That is very sweet of you." She opened the door. "Let me know if you need anything."

As soon as Tessa was out the door, I went to my desk and pulled up the number for my own realtor, who had helped me find my current location.

"Seth Crawford. How can I help you? Have you already grown out of your office building?"

I laughed. "No. I need help with something else."

I told him about the strip mall and asked him if he

could find out all the realtors who were working on deals there. "I'm specifically looking for someone who is helping a Tessa Archer and an Alexis. I'm sorry. I don't have her last name. If you can't find out the name of the real estate agent, can you give me a list, so I can call them myself?"

"Absolutely. Give me a couple of hours, and I'll get back to you."

"Call my cell, will you?"

"Sure will."

"Thank you."

I went back to what I had been working on before Tessa showed up, and I got a call about an hour later. Because it was less time than he had said, I was prepared to write down a list of names.

"What do you have for me?" I asked.

"Jana Symes is who you're looking for."

"This is who is helping Tessa and Alexis?"

"The one and only. And Alexis's last name is Moore. I emailed you their realtor's contact information."

"You are awesome. Thank you."

"Glad I could help."

I hung up the phone and called Jana Symes.

"This is Jana."

"Hi, Jana. My name is Seth Crawford, and I need the phone number of one of your clients. An Alexis Moore. Can you get me in touch with her, please?"

Chapter Twenty-Nine

SETH

I STOOD up from the small table in the back of the coffee shop when I saw Tessa's friend Alexis walk through the door.

"Hello," she said when she approached me.

"Please sit," I said.

When I had asked her to meet with me and not tell Tessa, she'd been very skeptical, not that I blamed her. But when I'd told her that I wanted to help her with her business and that we'd be in public, she'd agreed to meet me.

Alexis eyed me up and down, and I could tell she was uneasy, so I leaned back to keep my distance, hopefully making her feel more at ease.

"What can I help you with?" she asked.

"Nothing. It's me who wants to help you."

"How so?"

"Tessa told me about the building you want to buy and

what happened. I also know that you don't have enough money for a down payment to secure your loan."

"That's correct."

"I want to help with that."

She narrowed her eyes. "So, why aren't you talking to Tessa instead of me?"

I sighed. "Because Tessa won't let me help her."

Alexis looked away, and some of the stiffness in her posture disappeared. She turned back to me. "That sounds like her."

"I offered to give her the money, and she said no. Then, I offered to loan her the money, and she still said no."

"I'm not surprised."

"I take it, she didn't tell you?"

Alexis shook her head. "No."

Now, I was the one who was not surprised.

"Look, I don't want to get in between you as partners or friends, but I care about Tessa, and I want to help."

Alexis didn't respond right away. I let her think it over. But finally, she said, "What are you thinking?"

"Let me give you the money."

Alexis winced.

"I don't want to sound like an asshole, but when I say that I can afford it, trust me, I can afford it. It seems like such a waste to have money and not be able to help my friends."

Alexis chuckled. "Tessa's a friend now?"

I smiled. "Yes...and then some," I admitted. "And hopefully, this means you and I will be friends too."

"I appreciate it, but it's not just the amount. I understand that you have cash to spare, but it's also going behind my friend's back and not telling her. And while I wish she had told me about your proposal, I can't just take money from you. It doesn't feel right. Even if we are friends."

"A loan then? I won't charge any interest."

Alexis chewed on her lip. "I don't know. How am I going to pay you back and pay the mortgage? And where am I going to tell Tessa I got the money? She won't go through with it if she knows it's from you."

At least she was seriously considering the options I had given her.

"I think I have an idea on how we can manage this."

Alexis leaned forward. "What's your idea?"

Tessa

The following Monday, I was only at work for about an hour when Alexis called me on my cell.

"Hello?"

"Can you meet me at the realtor's office in about an hour?"

"Why? What's going on?"

"I'll explain when we get there. Now, can you get away?"

I looked over at Seth's open door. "I don't know. I guess I can ask. What about you?"

"My boss already gave me the okay."

"Hold on. I'll ask." I pressed my phone to my chest and went to Seth's office. "Seth?"

He looked up. "Yes?"

"I'm not sure what is going on, but Alexis asked if I could meet her in about an hour. I know you have a meeting at ten, so if you need me there, I'll let her know."

The truth was, I wanted Seth to tell me I couldn't go. I didn't need any more disappointment.

"It's fine." He smiled. "I'll make Jayden take notes."

"Are you sure? I can stay if you—"

"Tessa."

"What?"

"It's fine. Just go."

"Okay." I lifted the phone. "Alexis?"

"Yeah?"

"I'll be there."

"Wonderful. See you then."

An hour later, I pulled into the parking lot of our realtor's office. Alexis's car was already there, but she wasn't in it, so she must have gone into the building.

When I walked in, the receptionist at the front seemed to already be expecting me because she stood and said, "Right this way."

I nodded a thank-you when I reached the realtor's door.

Alexis and Jana looked up when they saw me.

"Come in," Jana said and got up to close the door behind me.

"What's going on?" I asked. "Did the other buyer pull out?"

"No," Jana said. "But Alexis called me this morning and said you two want to put in an official offer."

I sat next to Alexis and looked at her like she was crazy. "But we talked about this. We don't have the funds."

She smiled. "I came into some money."

I gasped. "Oh my God, he sold the house," I said, referring to her ex.

"Uh...no, not quite."

"Then, how?"

"Someone came to me and offered to give us the cash we needed up front, and in return, they would be a silent investor."

"Who is it?"

Alexis shrank into herself. "I can't say."

"What?" I shook my head. "Then, I'm not doing it."

Jana stood again. "Let me give you two a minute to discuss."

Once we were alone, Alexis turned from meek to angry. "So, because you say no, that's it? We don't even get to talk about it? I thought this business relationship was fifty-fifty."

Ouch. She had me there.

"You're right. And I'm sorry. I just don't trust this when I don't know who is giving us the money."

"But *I* know. *I* know who is giving us the money. And I wouldn't do this unless I trusted them."

"Then, why can't I know who they are?"

"Because this is between me and them, and they asked me to keep this information private."

"What do they get out of it?" I asked, figuring whoever this individual was, they were trying to scam us.

"One percent of our gross."

"One percent?" I scoffed. "I don't believe it."

"Well, start. That was the term we agreed upon."

"That's barely anything."

"They're not doing it for the money. They're doing it to help us."

I eyed Alexis. "It's not your ex, is it?" I really hoped she hadn't asked that guy out of desperation.

Alexis laughed. "I can't get him to sell our house. Why would he give me money?"

"I don't know. Maybe so you wouldn't force him to sell the house."

She would get more money from the sale of the house than from making up the difference in our down payment.

"Oh. Yeah, that makes sense, but no. I would never ask him for anything."

"Good." I tried to think of whoever else in Alexis's life would loan her the money, but I couldn't come up with anyone who had the funds. Unless it was someone who did but didn't want others to know. I chewed on my lip. That was a very real possibility.

Once my brother and I had moved out, my parents had

had more money for themselves. They paid off their home a couple of years ago and were able to save quite a bit of money, but they hadn't gone around flaunting it or even telling others. My mom had a brother who was always broke, and if he knew about the savings, he would hit up my mom constantly. Alexis's silent investor might have a similar situation.

"Are you sure we can trust this person?"

"Yes. They even had their lawyer draw up papers."

I frowned. "Their lawyer?"

Alexis laughed, but it seemed forced. "Oh, you know, a lawyer they paid."

I didn't know if she was hiding something or if she was worried I'd say no, but I really wanted to believe her.

"Okay, let's do this."

Alexis clapped her hands. "*Yes.*"

Two hours later, I hugged Alexis, got in my car, and called Seth.

"Seth Crawford."

"Hey, it's me."

"Who's me?"

I laughed. "Your assistant."

"Oh yeah, I almost forgot about you; you've been gone so long."

"You told me I could go."

He chuckled. "You're right; I did. I'm just teasing, I

promise. Are you calling to tell me you're not coming back?"

"Nope. I'm calling to ask you to go to dinner with me tonight to celebrate."

"What are we celebrating?"

"Alexis found an investor. We put in an offer for the store, and it was accepted."

"Congratulations. This is great news."

I breathed a sigh of relief. A part of me had worried he'd be upset that I had accepted this arrangement and not the one he'd offered me.

"It is. So, what do you say to dinner?"

"I say yes. But..." Seth trailed off.

"But what?"

"It's lunchtime. Why don't we celebrate with lunch and dinner?"

"Okay. Where are we going?"

"You pick where we go for dinner, and I pick where we go for lunch."

"Deal. We're going somewhere fancy for dinner."

"I would hope so. We're celebrating."

"Great. I'll let you know where once I decide." I laughed. "But until then, where are we going for lunch?" I asked.

"My place. I want you naked and on my bed within the half hour."

Chapter Thirty

TESSA

"I WISH I could go out of town with you again." I stuck out my lower lip, pretending that I was pouting.

Seth swung his office chair around, picked me up by my hips, and set me down on his desk in front of him. "Me too."

I looked over my shoulder just to make sure his office door was closed.

I was now on my ninth week here, and we tried not to mess around at work. But I hadn't seen him last night, and today, he was getting on a plane in a few hours. It was our last chance to see each other before he left for the weekend.

I cupped his face. "Where are you going again?" I already knew the answer, but I wanted to tease him for not taking me. "To meet Ryan Jackman in person?"

He drew me down for a kiss. "You know I'm going to

Chicago to meet up with an old client. If I meet Ryan Jackman, I will make sure you are there with me."

"You're the best boss ever."

He smirked. "In that case, I think I deserve a treat before I go."

"What do you have in mind?"

"Lie back."

I did as he'd said, resting on my elbows.

Seth pushed my skirt up and pulled my panties down and off. "I'm taking these with me."

My jaw dropped. "You are not. I can't walk around the rest of the day with no underwear."

"Fine. But then you have to let me have a taste." He tugged me to the edge of the desk and put his mouth on my pussy. He licked each side and circled my clit with his tongue, not quite hitting it. "Damn, you taste extra good today." He flicked my sweet spot before I could even say *thank you.*

"I thought you wanted a treat for you? This feels like a treat for me."

"It's a treat for both of us."

Since we'd been sleeping together for weeks now, he knew all the ways to bring me to orgasm, and since we were in his office, I didn't blame him for wanting to get to the final act.

He pushed two fingers into me and hooked them toward himself. The double stimulation was a good way to make me come, and within a few minutes, I was shoving my fist against my mouth to prevent my cries from escaping the room as I came.

Seth stood, grabbed a condom from his desk drawer, yanked it on, and thrust inside me. "I will never get used to how good you feel."

I moaned. "You don't have to flatter me with compliments. You're already inside me."

He laughed. "Maybe I'm just making sure I get to do this when I come back." He pulled back and pushed back in.

I was sensitive from my orgasm, and I couldn't help but squirm. "Go faster."

"Faster?"

"And harder."

He dropped his body down over mine. "Are you sure?" he asked with a twinkle in his eye.

He already knew I liked it when he rammed into me over and over again if we had sex after I already came.

"You're right; I changed my mind. Go nice and slow," I teased.

"If you say so," he said, calling my bluff.

He gently withdrew and slowly pressed back into me. He took his sweet time, and I wanted him to pick up the pace, but I didn't want to be the one to give in.

"If you don't hurry, you're going to be late."

He smiled and kissed me. "I have time."

His dick dragged against my sides, and I wanted to scream.

Finally, I couldn't stand it anymore. "Please, Seth, I need it."

"Need what, Tessa?"

"Your cock. The way I like it."

"And how do you like it?"

"Deep, deep inside me."

"All you had to do was ask." Seth cupped the back of my neck and pounded into me.

"Yes." I clutched his ass. "Yes, please."

He gave me everything I wanted, and my eyes started to roll back in my head as I felt another orgasm building.

"Tessa, I want you to come with me."

I nodded.

"Can you come now?"

I shook my head all of two times before I exploded.

"Liar," he said and slammed into me one last time.

We were both breathing heavy, and it took us a minute before Seth was able to stand up off of me.

"Fuck, I am going to miss you while I'm gone."

I laughed and straightened my skirt. "Where's my underwear?"

Seth picked them up and handed them to me before taking off the rubber. He pulled his pants back up and collapsed in his chair.

"Are you sure you're not just going to miss all the sex we have?" I asked as I pulled on my panties and stood.

"I don't know. Are you going to miss me or my dick?" he asked with a smile.

"Both."

"Honest answer—I like that. I'll miss both of you too."

"Both?"

"Yes. You and your pussy."

"Ah. Got it."

"Do you blame me? We've had six weeks of uninterrupted naked time. Or has it been only five?"

"Somewhere around there," I said, not wanting to do the math at the moment. "Are you sure you don't need me to take you to the airport?"

"No, the car service is already coming."

"When?"

He looked at his watch. "Shit. In about five minutes."

"Five minutes?"

"Yeah, I need to stop by the cemetery to see John on my way to the airport."

Disappointment hit me. I knew that Seth's partner had died and that he went to see him every month on a Friday, but he never opened up about what had happened to his friend. And he never asked me to go with him. This would be his third visit since I'd started working there and his second since we'd started sleeping together.

I kept telling myself and my friends that this fling we had together would end soon after I quit, but it hadn't stopped me from developing feelings for him. I liked him. A whole lot. And while I'd tried to resist him, I also hadn't stopped the whole affair. It was one of those relationships I wanted to look back on with a smile.

None of my resistance could have prevented me from feeling unhappy, but it probably just proved that we weren't meant to last forever because if we were, he would open up to me about John.

"You'd better get going then. You don't want to miss your flight."

Seth stood, cupped my cheeks, and kissed me. "I sure am going to miss you."

"You too."

"Don't have too much fun without me."

"I won't. Alexis and I will just be planning for our move-in date in a few weeks," I said. It was just in time for Seth's assistant to come back to work.

Despite my discontent with Seth leaving, I couldn't help but feel happy with the bakery and café. Construction was almost done, and we were closing in a couple weeks. I couldn't wait to get in there and decorate the place.

He scanned my face. "Take care, okay?"

I tilted my head. He seemed so sad. "I will. You too. Fly safe."

"I will." He dropped a peck on my forehead, grabbed his suitcase by the couch, and was out the door.

I ambled back to my desk in no hurry. It was Friday afternoon, I'd just had a wonderful orgasm, and the boss had left for the weekend. I didn't want to do any more work.

I laid my head down on my arms for a second, ready to take a nap when I heard voices and snapped up. If I fell asleep, I wouldn't have anyone to wake me up like Seth had all those weeks ago. But the good thing was, I probably wouldn't have any nightmares. I hadn't had one for over a month, although lately, I'd been so tired that I couldn't remember having any dreams at all.

Forcing myself to get something done before I went home for the day, I woke up my computer and looked at the time in the corner. Along with the time was the date, and I remembered what Seth had said about being together, so I thought I'd count the weeks.

Really, I was procrastinating about accomplishing any more work, but I figured it would be fun to check.

We'd slept together on the second night of our trip, which was…over six weeks ago.

Wow. Six weeks.

I frowned. *Wait a minute…*

Seth had said, "We've had six weeks of uninterrupted naked time."

Six weeks of *uninterrupted* naked time.

I gasped. *Shit.*

Chapter Thirty-One
TESSA

MONDAY MORNING, I dreaded coming into work.

I hadn't seen Seth since he'd left town. He had gotten back last night, and I had invited him over, knowing we had to have a talk, but he'd told me he was too tired.

So, today, I had to make the decision of either dropping the bomb on him while I was at the office or I had to keep it to myself all day. There was no way he wasn't going to want to be alone with me after we hadn't seen each other for a few days.

Although he hadn't wanted to see me last night, so maybe he wouldn't have time.

I tried to feel hopeful that today would go well, but I couldn't.

I was panicking about our forthcoming conversation. I was feeling insecure because he hadn't come over last night, and it was a Monday. I wanted it to be last Friday before Seth ever left.

I was so lost in my own thoughts that I almost missed the woman sitting at my desk.

"Oh, hello," I said. I didn't recognize her, and I hoped she wasn't someone who was digging around in my stuff when all she had to do was ask me for something.

The woman had long blonde hair, which she whipped over her shoulder at the sound of my voice.

I didn't know what I'd expected, but it wasn't the grin showing on the woman's face.

She stood up and hugged me. "Oh my God, it's so nice to meet you," she said.

"Um, it's nice to meet you too." Except for one thing. "And you are?"

She laughed, the sound melodic. "You're so funny. I'm Jill."

I was taken aback. "Oh. Jill." Seth's assistant. His regular, full-time assistant.

"Oh gosh, did Seth not tell you I was coming back early?"

"No. I'm sorry. I would have gotten my stuff out of the way if I had known."

She waved off my apology. "It's no bother." She shook her head. "And I should have known to tell you myself that I was coming back. I just asked him last night when he came over if he'd told you. I could have sworn he said yes, but you know how men are when they have their mind on something else."

Seth had gone to her place last night. And I could only guess what the *something else* was.

I think I'm going to be sick.

"Yeah," I said. "Do you know where Seth is?"

She sighed and shook her head. "It's a good thing I'm back because that man doesn't tell you anything, does he? He left town again early this morning." She rolled her eyes. "I feel like he's always busy with something."

My heart was pounding, and my vision wasn't so good.

"Oh my," Jill said. "You look like you could use a chair." She pushed hers toward me. "Here, sit in mine."

I collapsed onto the leather, closed my eyes, and took a couple of deep breaths. But all I kept hearing was how Seth had gone to her place. He'd lied to me.

If Jill wasn't so nice, I would punch her in the face.

Although she seemed as if she knew nothing about me besides me being his temporary assistant.

"How long have you known Seth?" I asked.

"We've been together for over ten years. Can you believe it?"

Ten years? It was worse than I'd thought.

I shook my head because I couldn't form any words.

"How was it while I was gone?" she asked. "I heard you got to go to San Francisco. How was that?"

I gave her a thumbs-up.

"I love going to California, but I did get to do something a little more exciting. Do you want to see?"

Since I wasn't sure my legs would hold me up yet, I nodded because it was the polite thing to do.

Jill picked up her phone, swiped a few times, and showed me a picture of a newborn.

Oh shit. I'd forgotten she'd been out on maternity leave. *Does Seth have a baby with her?*

I felt like I was going to throw up again.

She slid through quite a few pictures, and I couldn't tell much. The baby was a newborn, but as the images showed him starting to get older, I couldn't stop the sinking feeling in my gut.

I wanted her to keep going but to also stop and not show me one more photo.

So, when she did pause and look at me, I wanted to scream.

"Did Seth go and visit John while I was gone?"

I nodded.

"Oh good. Sometimes, I would have to bug him to go, and I was so worried he wouldn't. And I didn't put it in my notes for you because it's so personal." She leaned forward. "Not everyone here knows that his old partner hanged himself and left Seth to find him."

I thought I'd stopped breathing. That was what had happened with his old partner? And he never told me? I'd practically had to prod him to tell me John had died.

Jill put her hand on my shoulder. "I'm glad he had someone like you to fill in while I was gone. I know he really liked having you here."

You wouldn't be so glad if you knew that I was sleeping with him, lady. And, yeah, he liked having me here but not enough to open up about John, not enough to tell me you were coming back, and not enough to tell me he was already in a relationship, apparently.

Maybe they weren't really in a relationship. Maybe I was jumping to conclusions.

"Do you have any more pictures?"

Jill laughed. "Oh, yeah." She held up her cell again and flipped through the images. The further she went, the more the baby looked like Seth.

"He's...beautiful," I managed to say.

"Thank you." She hugged her phone to her chest. "We named him Declan Seth so that he could be named after—"

I jumped up from the chair and almost knocked Jill over.

This time, I really was going to be sick. I barely made it to the restroom before I threw up.

It seemed that Seth had a thing where he dated his assistants and got them pregnant.

And nothing would probably ever happen with him because he was a rich guy. I should have listened to my instincts when it came to a man with money because, now, I was starting a business and going to have a baby. Alone.

I used toilet paper to wipe my face, rinsed my mouth out at the sink, and left the Bradford Group without even taking my stuff. I never wanted to see the place again.

Chapter Thirty-Two
TESSA

TWO MONTHS LATER

ALEXIS AND I STOOD, arm in arm, outside The Purrfect Café & Bakery and watched as my brother put up a Grand Opening sign.

"I can't believe today is the day," Alexis said.

"Me neither. We couldn't have asked for better weather."

It was fall in Minnesota, so the trees were red, yellow, and orange, but the weather was relatively warm for the time of year.

"Cold enough for people to want coffee but not cold enough for them to stay home."

I laughed. "We can only hope."

Zack looked down from his ladder at me. "How does that look?"

"It's crooked," I told him.

"Still?"

"She's teasing you, Zack," Alexis said. "It's flawless."

My brother narrowed his eyes at me. "You're lucky I'm up here and you're down there."

I waved him away. "You wouldn't hurt me." I tugged on Alexis's arm. "Come on. Let's see how they're doing inside."

Once through the door, I couldn't help but stop and admire the place. It was everything I'd dreamed it would be. We had a state-of-the-art espresso machine, a beautiful bakery case, and six cats who needed homes. It was perfect.

One of the cats, a calico named Spice, rubbed up against me at the same time I noticed Elizabeth sitting at the counter, looking sad.

I picked up Spice and made my way over to my friend. "Hey, are you okay?"

"Yeah, I'm fine," she said but didn't look at me.

I followed her gaze to where Isabelle was talking to Sebastian, Bree's cousin who'd just moved back to Minnesota.

"Is everything alright?"

Elizabeth looked at me and sighed. "Yeah." She smiled. "But even if it wasn't, this is your big day. Not mine."

"Hey, you're important. Alexis and I couldn't have done this without you." And I wouldn't have made it the last two months, missing Seth, without them either.

Seth had called and messaged me after I left the Bradford Group. He had gotten to his new destination on the trip I hadn't even known about, and he'd told me he was sorry he'd had to leave so soon.

I didn't respond because I didn't want to get into it with him. I erased his texts, ignored his calls, blocked his phone number, and deleted his contact information.

A couple weeks later, I got my last paycheck and a glowing recommendation. I'd quit the temp agency that same day.

No job was worth the heartache because I hadn't realized how much I cared about Seth until I found out he didn't care about me.

My only regret was not telling Jill that her boyfriend and the father of her child was a snake. I'd thought about going back and telling her, but it wasn't worth the risk of running into Seth.

At least, not at this time. After the baby was born, there was a chance I'd feel differently.

I rubbed my belly. I was just hitting my second trimester and thankfully not showing. My friends knew, and so did my parents and brother. But I hadn't told anyone else as of yet. And I still didn't know if I was going to tell Seth.

I knew it was the right thing to do, but I didn't want his money or child support. And I was afraid with his money, he'd be able to take the baby away from me.

Ugh. I couldn't think about that now.

I shook off any sad thoughts and focused on the good news of today.

And when the door opened and Pru walked in with the stools I'd ordered, it gave me something else to do.

"Thank you for picking these up," I said to her, taking one of them from her.

"You're welcome."

"Is the third one in your car?"

"No. A nice gentleman helped me bring the last one in."

At the word *gentleman*, my heart skipped a beat, but the man walking into the café was no one I'd seen before.

Isabelle made a sound and came bouncing over to us. "You made it," she said to the guy.

He smiled at her. "I did." He looked at me. "I hope it's okay that I'm here. I'm willing to help. Just put me to work."

"Thank you for the offer," I said. "But Isabelle hasn't told us who you are."

Isabelle blushed and waved her hand. "Everyone, this is Jamie...the guy I'm seeing."

The room erupted in cheers until the sound of a loud bang made us all turn and look.

Elizabeth was picking up the stool she'd been sitting on. She held up her hand. "Sorry. Don't mind me." She set it under the counter and went out the back door.

"What's that about?" Pru asked me.

"I don't know, but she seems sad today."

"I'll go have a talk with her."

"Good idea."

"Can I put those away for you?"

We turned to see Sebastian standing there.

"Thank—" I started to say when Pru cut me off.

"What are you doing here?" she asked.

"*Pru.* Sebastian was kind enough to come and help today."

She curled her lip. "I meant, what is he doing in Minnesota?"

Sebastian grinned at her. "I live here."

"Ugh," Pru said with an eye roll. She snatched the stool out of my hands and took it over to the empty counter.

"Jeez, she doesn't care much for you, does she?" I said to Sebastian.

He shrugged. "I'll grow on her."

I doubted that, but then again, I didn't know what the animosity between them was about. Besides, I had a grand opening I needed to worry about.

Chapter Thirty-Three

TESSA

SEVERAL HOURS into the grand opening, everything was going smoothly. In my mind, I'd always pictured a line of people waiting to get in, going around the corner, but in reality, it was more of a steady flow, which made it a lot easier to keep the customers happy.

I finished ringing up a customer and was putting their money in the cash register when the next person stepped up.

"Hello. Is there something I can get for you?" I asked without looking up.

"Two lemon cupcakes, please."

I froze.

I knew that voice.

I finished sliding the bills in the right slots and looked up, coming face-to-face with Seth...who was holding the baby boy from Jill's pictures. The baby looked so much like him.

It hurt my heart to see this, but it also made my hormones go, *Look, he's a good daddy.* He also looked sexy as hell in his jeans and T-shirt. Man, oh man, did I miss him.

"Hi, Tessa."

I couldn't do this. Not here and not today.

"Paisley?" I called.

She was only a few feet away, speaking with a customer.

"Yeah?"

"Can you come take over for me? I need to step out."

"Sure."

Thank God for amazing friends.

Paisley walked around the corner, and her eyes widened when she saw Seth but only for a second. She managed to compose herself right away. "What can I get you?" she asked him.

"He wants two lemon cupcakes."

Her eyes darted to me and back to Seth. By now, she had heard the whole story of Alexis bringing the cupcakes to work.

"I'll be back in five," I told her, hoping she knew it might be longer than that, depending on how long Seth stuck around.

I slipped off my apron and headed for the back of the store. It was where we kept a room just for the cats' litter boxes and where the office was.

"I'll be right back," I heard Seth say behind me.

I picked up my pace, but he caught up to me and put his hand on my arm.

"Tessa, please, can we talk?"

I slowly pivoted. "Today? Now?"

"You blocked my phone number. I knew you would be here today."

Okay, he had me there, but I didn't want to do this right now. I looked around the room, trying to figure out what to do. I could tell him we'd meet later, but I knew I would ruminate over it the rest of the day. If we talked right here, right now, I could get it over with.

"Fine." There was an empty table, and I went to sit down.

Seth sat across from me, and the baby on his lap immediately slammed his hands down on the table and made cute baby noises.

I couldn't help but smile at the little guy, and I realized he was going to be my baby's half-brother. That seemed unreal.

"Okay, what do you want to talk about?" I asked Seth when he didn't say anything right away.

"First things first. I'm sorry."

I snorted. "What for exactly?"

Seth opened his mouth, but then the baby reached back and tried to grab Seth's face. He sighed. "Hold on." He picked up his phone, hit a button, and put it to his ear. A few seconds later, he said, "I need you to come in here and get your kid. He's a menace."

My jaw dropped.

Seth had said it in a joking tone, but that didn't matter. I couldn't believe he'd talked to the mother of his child like that.

He laughed at something and added, "Next time, I'm charging you money when you ask me to babysit."

This was so different from the Seth I knew. A man didn't babysit his own kids.

Maybe this conversation would be easier than I'd thought. I was feeling less hurt and more relieved with each word he spoke. Maybe I had dodged a bullet.

He hung up the phone, and I was about ready to tell him that he was an asshole to Jill when she walked in and scooped the baby up from the table.

"Declan, are you being a troublemaker?"

The baby laughed.

"Sorry, Seth. We didn't realize we were outside, talking that long."

"It's okay," he said.

Between this whole exchange, my head was going from one to the other. Why wasn't Jill mad at him? And the more I thought about it, why was she okay with him sitting and talking to me?

I was just about to tell Jill she had nothing to apologize for when someone came up behind her and pulled the baby from her arms.

The man stepped around Jill, and I gasped.

The guy looked so much like Seth that they had to be brothers, and for a moment, I thought they might be twins with different haircuts.

The man noticed me and said, "You must be Tessa."

I nodded slowly.

"I'm Dex."

I held my hand out. "Hi, Dex," I said in a daze. "You must be Seth's brother?"

Dex shot Seth a look. "Holy shit, man, do you not tell this woman anything?" He turned back to me. "Yes, I'm his brother." He put his arm around Jill. "And this one's husband." He pulled his arm from Jill and tickled the baby's stomach. "And this guy's daddy."

So many things clicked into place. Why Seth had gone to Jill's after his flight. He'd actually gone over to his brother's. And the baby looked like him because he was the uncle. It also explained the joking tone when he was on the phone. He'd been teasing his brother, not talking to the mother of his child.

At this point, I felt like everything I knew had been turned upside down. Kind of like it had the day I walked out of the Bradford Group.

"We'll leave you two to talk," Dex said as he and Jill walked away.

"So, Jill is married to your brother?"

Seth smiled. "Yeah. I introduced them to each other. They named Declan after me because of that. His middle name anyway."

If I had known this, it would have made my life a lot easier a couple of months ago.

"Why didn't you tell me about your brother?"

"I don't know. We didn't talk about our families a

whole lot." He shrugged. "I always had a sense that you had an expiration date on our relationship, and that's why we never talked about things like that."

I cleared my throat and looked away.

"But after you left the company, I realized that I didn't want things to end. I wanted to be with you even if you weren't working for me."

"Is that why you never told me about John?"

He looked surprised.

"Jill told me he died by suicide, but whenever I'd asked you about him, you'd shut me down."

"Because I feel guilty." Seth leaned forward, resting his elbows on his knees. "John and I were gaining momentum with our new business when a company came to us about advertising. The company was big, so I was excited. Not only would they be able to pay us well, but if they used us, it would also get our name out there."

I could understand that.

"John asked me not to go through with it. They were homophobic, and he was gay. This was news to me. On both fronts. John had never told me his sexual orientation, and I had never heard of this company doing anything homophobic, so even though John had asked me not to do business with them, I insisted we give them a chance, and he reluctantly agreed."

I already had a feeling of where this was going.

"John wasn't happy with me for weeks, but he willingly made an effort with the company." Seth took a deep breath. "But John's friends and his boyfriend, who I had just found out about, discovered who he was doing business with. They basically disowned him, and his boyfriend broke up with him."

Poor John.

"He didn't tell me any of this was happening, and I thought he had been having a rough couple of days. But then the president of marketing of their company told John that either he quit or they were taking their business elsewhere. I didn't find that out until after John died. He had sacrificed everything for our business. For this company to turn around and tell him he had to quit the agency he'd started pushed him past his limit."

I felt so bad for John. And for Seth.

"I knew that John had bouts of depression, but I didn't know how bad it was. And this whole mess broke him. I found him at his home." Seth cleared his throat. "It was the worst thing I've seen in my life." He looked up at me. "And I really don't want to talk about it."

"It's okay. I understand."

"I actually thought about quitting after that, but I didn't. Instead, I fired the company and made sure that other potential clients knew where I stood when it came to LGBTQIA rights. I also learned that I needed to expand my horizons and that just because something doesn't happen to me or just because I don't see it, it doesn't mean it's not a problem or it doesn't happen. That's why I have no patience for people like Gene Ainsworth. He's a bully and an asshole."

"Thank you for telling me. You didn't have to do that."

Chapter Thirty-Four

SETH

"I KNOW I didn't have to, but I wanted to. I want you to know how important you are to me."

I had missed Tessa the last two months. When she ignored my calls and texts, I started kicking myself for giving Alexis the money for their bakery. I had known she didn't want my money to help, but I'd had no idea she was going to cut me out of her life like that.

"You might think differently after I tell you how big I messed up."

Wait. She messed up? I thought I was the one who had messed up.

"It can't be that bad."

She cringed. "I thought you were sleeping with Jill and had a baby with her all the while you were sleeping with me," she spat out rapid-fire.

"Wow." I hadn't expected that. "*That's* the reason you ghosted me?"

"Yes," she admitted reluctantly.

"You actually thought I was that kind of person?" It would be funny if it didn't hurt so much.

"I mean...no. But when I met Jill, she started talking about you going to her house the night before. You'd already told me you were too tired to come over. And then she showed me pictures of a baby who looked just like you and had your name as his middle name."

"You didn't think to ask more questions?"

"I thought she was your girlfriend or something. I wasn't going to let her know the father of her child was sleeping with someone else."

I ran my hands over my face in frustration. "Okay, but you could have asked me about it."

She hung her head. "You're right. I should have done that, and I was wrong. My only excuse is that I need to get over my plutophobia, but it's just that—an excuse. I should have trusted you, and I should have trusted my feelings for you."

I leaned forward and took her hands. "First, we all make mistakes. And second, what is plutophobia?"

That got her to smile, and it made me feel good to see that. "It's fear of wealth."

"They have a word for that?"

"They have a word for everything." She met my eyes. "I'm sorry. If it helps, I feel like a total fool."

I scoffed. "No, I don't want you to feel like a fool." I tugged on her arms to get her to stand and pulled her onto my lap. "I love you, and even though I'm hurt you would think those things about me, I don't want you to hurt too."

Her eyes widened. "You..." She took a deep breath. "You love me?"

"Yes. I wouldn't have crashed just anyone's grand opening."

She flung her arms around my neck and hugged me. She rested her head on my shoulder. "I think I love you too."

Rubbing her back, I asked, "You think?"

"My brain is still processing everything. I know I've missed you, more than I can hardly believe, and if I didn't care about you, I wouldn't have been so upset about what I thought I had found out."

Surprisingly, this did make me feel better.

"I'm glad you missed me."

"I'm so sorry I jumped to the wrong conclusions and didn't talk to you."

"I'm sorry, too, but I'm glad we're talking now."

Tessa lifted her head. "That's the second time you've apologized. What did you do wrong?" she asked with a laugh.

"You know, giving the money to Alexis to secure this place. I knew you wouldn't be thrilled, and this whole time, I thought that's what you were mad at me about. I'm so relieved you're not."

She held up her finger. "Hold that thought." She jumped off my lap and called out, "Alexis, can you come over here?"

She was bringing drinks over to some customers, and once she set them down, she came over to us. "Seth," she said with her eyes wide. "You two are talking again."

"Yes, I'll explain later," Tessa said. "I was all wrong about him and Jill. But the important thing I need to know right now is, did Seth give you money?"

Alexis bit her lip.

"That's a yes," Tessa said. "Alexis, why?"

"Because we needed the money, Seth was willing to help, and I went into it with a clear head."

"You did?"

"Yes. Your fears and your feelings for Seth were clouding your judgment. But I'm not afraid of rich people, and I barely know Seth. Plus, we had a lawyer set up everything with legal documents." She crossed her arms over her chest. "I stand by my decision. Seth's a good guy and probably the best investor we could have asked for."

Tessa looked at me.

"She's right. I am a good guy. Also, I'm such a good investor that you can keep your one percent of the profits. I did it for you, not the money."

"Aww..." Alexis dropped her arms. "Tessa, if what you're saying about being wrong is true, you need to marry this man right away. He's the sweetest."

"Did you hear that? I'm the sweetest."

Tessa rolled her eyes. "You two need to get a room."

Alexis laughed. "You're funny, but I'm still part of the club, unlike you."

Tessa's mouth fell open. "How rude."

"What club is this?" I asked.

"The United She-Woman Single Ladies with Our Vibrators So We Never Have Another Bad Date or Experience Romance Again Because Men Suck Club," Alexis said.

My brow flew up. "That's quite a mouthful."

"That's what she said," a guy said as he happened to be walking by and heard my comment.

A woman coming from the other direction said, "What is *wrong* with you?"

"Wouldn't you like to know?" he retorted and kept walking.

I burst out laughing. "Do you know those two?"

"Yes," Alexis answered. "The woman is our friend Pru, and the guy, Sebastian, is a cousin of another friend of ours."

"I'd like to meet the rest of your friends," I told Tessa. "That is, if you'll have me," I teased.

Alexis rolled her eyes. "Tessa will get over you being our silent investor. She likes you way too much to hold a grudge over a little thing like money."

I grinned.

"Plus, you two are having a baby together. You're going to be exchanging a lot more than money in the future."

I furrowed my brow and tilted my head. "I'm sorry. I think I misheard you."

Tessa closed her eyes and shook her head while Alexis's eyes got as big as the cupcakes she made.

"I'm sorry. Someone needs me. Urgently. Gotta go." Alexis took off as fast as she could go.

I looked at Tessa. "Is there something else you need to tell me?"

She held up her hands. "Surprise, I'm pregnant."

I grabbed her waist and yanked her to me. I buried my face in her stomach. Even though I had teased my brother about coming to get Declan earlier, I really loved the little guy, and that little baby had made me realize how much I wanted kids someday.

I looked up at Tessa. "I'm going to be a father?"

She brushed her hand through my hair. "Is that okay?"

"More than. Marry me."

She gasped and laughed.

"I'm not joking. Marry me."

"Seth, we can't do that."

"Yes, we can. I love you, I want to be with you, and I want our baby to be with both of us."

"This is nuts."

"That's not a no," I pointed out.

"It's also not a yes."

"What's stopping you?" I brought her back down to my lap. "I'm serious. What's stopping you?"

"Won't people think it's too fast?"

"Who cares what other people think?"

"Even when it comes to your company? What if your clients think I'm a gold digger and that you're a fool for marrying me?"

"If you're worried, we'll do a prenup. As for what my

clients think, Tessa, you are way more important than my company or money. I'd rather be with you and broke than be without you and rich. I love you."

A tear slid down her cheek. "I love you too."

"Is that a yes?"

She nodded. "Yes."

I jumped up with Tessa cradled in my arms and shouted, "I'm getting married, and I'm going to be a father."

There was clapping and shouts of congratulations all around us. People took out their phones and snapped pictures of us.

I looked at Tessa and set her on her feet. "It looks like if I lose my company, The Purrfect Café and Bakery will keep us well fed."

"How do you know that?"

"By the number of people taking photos of us, we're going viral. Now, kiss me, so they have some good content to post on their social media."

Tessa smiled. "You are such a good advertiser."

"You know, if you need someone, I know a guy."

Chapter Thirty-Five

TESSA

"CLOSE YOUR EYES," Seth said.

I put my hand up, so I wouldn't see anything, and I felt him pick me up.

We'd gone to the courthouse to get married today with my brother and Seth's brother, Dex, as our witnesses.

I'd refused to have a big wedding. Not only did I not want to wait months to plan it with the baby coming, but I also didn't want people to think I was flaunting my soon-to-be husband's money. It was going to take time for me to get over my fears.

But I was getting better. Seth had indeed gotten his attorney to write up a prenuptial agreement, but the only thing that was on there was that if we divorced, The Purrfect Café and Bakery was all mine. I tried to say no, but he wanted me to feel secure and safe. He also pointed out that this way, if the press asked us about a prenuptial agreement, we wouldn't have to lie. I had reluctantly signed it but only because I planned to stay married to him forever.

And because I was trying to be better about Seth being able to afford things, I'd let him buy us a house. It had five bedrooms and four bathrooms, but it was around thirty years old. It needed some renovations, but I loved the feel of it, and as a bonus, we waited to elope until everything was finished, so we could move in.

I hadn't seen it for about a month because Seth wanted to surprise me, which was why I had my eyes closed as he carried me over the threshold.

"Okay, you can look."

I opened my eyes and gasped. "It's beautiful."

Everything was gleaming and looked up-to-date, but it also had a homey atmosphere. I'd made it absolutely known that I did not like the modern, sleek look. I wanted my children to grow up in a house that made them feel welcome. And Seth had delivered.

He set me on my feet as two figures came out from the adjacent room.

"My cats are already here," I said.

"Your friends brought them over. And all your stuff is moved in."

I turned around and kissed him. "I love it, husband."

"I'm glad you're happy, wife." He clasped my hand. "Come on. Let's go look around."

He led me upstairs and then downstairs, apparently saving the majority of the main floor for last.

When we got to the kitchen, there was a wrapped present on the counter.

"Seth, you didn't have to get me anything. Our wedding, this house, you—that's all I need."

He put his hands up. "It's not from me. But now, I feel like an ass for not getting you a present."

I kissed him. "I already told you, you're all the present I need."

There was a strong kick in my abdomen.

I looked down and rubbed my hand over my belly. "Yes, you're all the present I need too."

"I agree," Seth said, pulling me into his arms. "You two are all I need."

I turned so that my back was to him and picked up the present. It was a white box with a gift tag on it.

To: Tessa and Seth
From: Your business partner

"What would Alexis get us?" Seth asked.

I opened up the box and looked inside. "Oh my God. *Alexis.*"

Seth reached inside and pulled out a piping bag. "What is this?"

"Lemon frosting."

"Okay, now, you have to tell me what the inside joke is."

Epilogue

TESSA

ALEXIS SHIMMIED HER SHOULDERS. "Did you like my wedding gift?"

Bree gasped. "I *told* Zack we should get you a gift even though you told us 'absolutely not' and that you'd 'disown' us if we did."

I put my hand on Bree's arm. "Don't worry; it cost about a dollar to make."

"I'm with Bree," Pru said. "That's not right, especially after we talked about getting Tessa one big gift."

Alexis smiled. "I think you're going to have to tell the group what my gift to you was."

"Oh, yes," Paisley said. "You have to tell us."

I looked around the table at my friends. It was my first monthly dinner after becoming a married woman, and everyone wanted to know all the details of my life with my new husband.

"It was lemon frosting. That's it. Nothing big."

Isabelle scrunched up her nose. "Why lemon frosting?"

I told them all about when Seth had eaten the lemon cupcake at his office. "Alexis suggested I take lemon frosting on our business trip, so he could lick it off my body."

"And since she wouldn't take any on her trip to San Francisco, I thought it would be a perfect addition to a wedding night." Alexis grinned.

"So, did you like her gift?" Paisley asked.

I remembered how Seth had stripped off my dress and put frosting on my nipples before licking it off and then on my pussy before licking me clean. After he had given me my first orgasms as his wife, I'd covered his cock with the lemony goodness, so I could suck my husband off. It was a night I'd never forget.

"Yes, we both liked the gift. We baked our cupcakes and used the frosting."

Pru snorted. "Is that what you're calling sex now?"

Everyone broke out in laughter, including me.

"It's someone else's turn," I said. "No more about me."

Bree and Paisley started talking at the same time and both stopped.

"You go," Bree said.

"I don't want to. My news is not fun."

"Oh no," Elizabeth said. "What is it?"

"My landlord is going to sell my house." Paisley stuck

out her lip. "I love my house. The rent is cheap, and it's perfect for me."

"Can you buy it?" Isabelle asked. "It can't be that much to purchase."

Paisley shook her head. "No. It's going to be bulldozed and turned into a parking lot. Or something like that."

"Oof. That sucks," Isabelle said.

"It does. The worst part is, my landlord barely gave me any notice. I have to be out within two months. It seems like enough time, but it's really not when you have to find a place to live and then pack up your life to move."

"And I just sold my house," I said. "You could have bought mine or at least rented it, if we had known." My old place would have been perfect since I hadn't had to sell it for the money. I'd only sold it because Seth and I didn't need it anymore.

"Right?" Paisley said. "I doubt this deal is moving that fast. The a-hole probably didn't tell me until he absolutely had to."

"I don't have much to offer," Pru said. "But I can ask around."

"I can too," Bree said.

"Same here," Isabelle and Elizabeth said.

"I can have Seth ask at work too."

"Thanks, ladies. You're the best."

"That's what friends are for," I said.

"Enough about me. It's not the end of the world. If I have to move in with my parents, I will. I won't like it, but I will."

"Ugh," Bree said. "I don't blame you. I would not want to live with my mom. And too bad that Zack already told Sebastian he could stay at his place for now."

Pru looked at Bree. "He did?"

"Yeah. My cousin didn't want to live with his mom and dad either while he figures out where he wants to live permanently, and since Zack and I pretty much already live together, Zack let Sebastian rent his place."

"I'm glad you two have finally realized that you are going to spend the rest of your lives together," I said.

"I might have to admit it now," Bree said.

"Why now?" I asked.

Bree held up her left hand. "Because Zack asked me to marry him."

The group gasped and cheered.

I pulled Bree into an embrace. "We're officially going to be sisters-in-law."

She hugged me back. "It's pretty cool."

When we separated, Pru looked around the table. "Some man-haters club we are. One of us is married, and another is engaged. What's next?"

"Don't forget about Isabelle. She's dating someone too," Bree said.

I looked over to where Elizabeth was watching Isabelle, looking sad. "You okay, Elizabeth?"

She sat up in her seat. "What? Yeah, I'm okay. Just thinking about the group of us falling like dominoes."

I laughed. "It sure seems like it, huh?"

Paisley sighed. "I'm so jealous."

"*Paisley*," I teased. "Just say no."

She stuck her tongue out at me. "I know. I said I was on a man hiatus, and I meant it."

I laughed. *Famous last words.*

Turn the page for a sample of

NOT ANOTHER ONE-NIGHT STAND

Not Another One-Night Stand

COLIN

I dropped off my luggage in my hotel room and left to get a drink down at the hotel bar. Minnesota was six hours behind the UK, so it was the middle of the night there, but I had slept on the plane, and I wasn't ready to call it a night yet. I was hoping a little bit of alcohol would help me get some rest.

It was a Saturday night, so the bar was decently full but not too crowded, which I appreciated. I found a seat in the corner of the bar, where there were several empty stools. I was nursing my first drink when I saw her walk in.

She was average height, and the word *pretty* came to mind when describing her. But it was the red hair that really caught my eye. It was almost wild with curls going everywhere. She was dressed up, but she looked more like she was going to work rather than on a date, and she was alone. Her makeup was light, and her black dress had a modest neckline and three-quarter sleeves. The sexiest piece of clothing on her was her red heels.

She looked around, and I realized I might have been wrong. She could be meeting someone there, and maybe she liked to dress more conservatively for dates. Except her eyes scanned over all the people, and she only stopped when they landed on the empty stools next to me.

Her expression brightened, and she came and took the stool two away from mine. She gave me a polite smile, and I nodded in return before the bartender came over and took her drink order.

We both sat there, minding our own business for a good ten minutes before laughter had me looking up again. A group of women who I guessed to be in their mid-fifties walked in. And the redhead next to me stiffened. She slunk off her stool—there was no other way to describe it—and walked around to my side, facing the wall.

"I'm sorry to ask this," she whispered. "But can you move over one seat and let me take this spot? I'm hoping that won't be for long, but I would really appreciate it."

I moved over silently and let her take my old seat.

She sat down with a sigh. "Thank you."

"You're welcome." I tilted my head toward the ladies. "Not your friends, I take it?"

The redhead smiled. "I'm here for an office party. I just wanted to take a break for a little while, have a drink, and get away from everyone."

That explained the clothes and makeup. She actually was dressed for work instead of a night out.

I looked at the group of ladies, who were finding a table that, unfortunately, put the redhead and me in their line of view. I leaned forward, putting my elbows on the bar so that, hopefully, they wouldn't notice she was sitting next to me.

"So, those must be your coworkers?" I asked.

"Yes. The four of them work in the same area as me. They're nice enough, but they're not exactly the people I want to hang out with on a Saturday night." She chuckled. "That probably sounds mean, especially to someone who doesn't know me. I swear, I'm not a monster."

I offered her a reassuring smile. "I think we've all been there." I worked with several people who I wouldn't want to spend my time off with outside of work.

"Thank you. I'm the youngest of all of them by about twenty years. We're not at the same point in our lives, and they've all been working at the company a lot longer than me. Like I said, they're not my first pick of who I'd want to hang out with on a Saturday night." She took a sip of her drink. "Actually, I feel that way about my whole office. I work at a boring insurance company, so tonight's party isn't what I would call fun." She grinned. "Are you judging me yet?"

I laughed. "You don't have to justify anything to me. I'm just a stranger you met at the bar." But I felt like I needed to remedy that. I held out my hand. "I'm Colin, by the way."

Paisley

I smiled and said, "I'm Paisley," as I shook his hand.

Colin had blue eyes and blond hair and was the kind of guy most girls had a crush on in high school, including me. No surprise there. I'd had a crush on tons of guys in high school. I was me after all.

But being around someone so hot was not good for me and my *no men, no sex* rule.

Although...

"So, Colin, what brings you here tonight? Is it something as exciting as the sixtieth anniversary of your company being open?"

He grinned, which only made him more attractive. "I'm here for my job, too, and I actually have to do some work on Monday but nothing as exciting as an anniversary party." He snickered.

"You think you're funny, but if you had to be in that room with everyone from my office, you'd see how much work it actually is. And I'm not even getting paid for it."

He burst out laughing, and I wanted to give myself a pat on the back for making this beautiful man happy, if only for a moment.

He leaned closer to me. "You know, Paisley, I was regretting coming into town for a few days, but you might just change my mind."

"Might?"

He lifted his glass and emptied it. "We'll see how the rest of the night goes," he said, meeting my eyes.

Now that I knew he was only going to be in town for a few days, I had a good feeling on how the night would go.

It was going to end with the both of us naked.

About the Author

R.L. Kenderson is two best friends writing under one name.

Renae has always loved reading, and in third grade, she wrote her first poem where she learned she might have a knack for this writing thing. Lara remembers sneaking her grandmother's Harlequin novels when she was probably too young to be reading them, and since then, she knew she wanted to write her own.

When they met in college, they bonded over their love of reading and the TV show *Charmed*. What really spiced up their friendship was when Lara introduced Renae to romance novels. When they discovered their first vampire romance, they knew there would always be a special place in their hearts for paranormal romance. After being unable to find certain storylines and characteristics they wanted to read about in the hundreds of books they consumed, they decided to write their own.

One lives in the Minneapolis-St. Paul area and the other in the Kansas City area where they both work in the medical field during the day and a sexy author by night. They communicate through phone, email, and whole lot of messaging.

You can find them at http://www.rlkenderson.com, Facebook, Instagram, TikTok, and Goodreads. Join their reader group! Or you can email them at rlkenderson@rlkenderson.com, or sign up for their newsletter. They always love hearing from their readers.

Made in the USA
Columbia, SC
28 February 2024